THE FAR SANDS

Carol and Fay are identical twins. If Fay was capable of plotting and carrying out murder, which the coroner concludes she was, then is Carol?

James Renison has only recently married Carol and is in love with her, but he begins to worry for his own safety. He decides to dig deeper into the lives of his wife's family and sets out to establish for certain the identity of the killer who had struck on the Far Sands.

THE FAR SANDS

Andrew Garve

First published 1960
by
Harper & Brothers New York

This edition 2002 by Chivers Press
published by arrangement with
the author's estate

ISBN 0 7540 8611 9

Copyright © 1960 by Andrew Garve

British Library Cataloguing in Publication Data available

CHAPTER I

IT WAS Carol, I remembered afterwards, who made the initial advance and most of the running during the first few minutes of our acquaintance. The place was the little town of Boppard on the Rhine; the time, a spring-like Sunday morning in mid-March. I had just parked the Lagonda at the foot of the *sesselbahn* when the girl passed me on her way to join the queue at the ticket office. She looked at the big cream car admiringly, and then at me. As our eyes met she gave me a smile and said " Hallo " in an unmistakably English voice. I said " Hallo " back and gazed after her for a moment. From the brief glimpse I had had of her face she had seemed attractive. When, presently, I joined the queue myself, two portly German couples stood between us. With mild interest, I examined the girl over their heads. She had thick dark hair cropped in a carefully casual fashion and just clearing the collar of a scarlet windcheater. She wasn't very tall but she held herself well. Changing my position a little, I saw that she had extremely nice legs and ankles. Once she half-turned and caught my eye without apparent intention and smiled again. She *was* attractive. The queue moved forward and she bought her ticket and walked slowly up to the platform where the well-spaced chairs on their endless cable took on new passengers before starting to climb again. Chance, or perfect timing, found her at my side as one of the double chairs came swinging towards us. A blond youth helped her into the moving seat and motioned to me to take the place beside her. For a second I hesitated. " May I? " I asked. The girl said, " But of course," and I climbed in. A moment later we had cleared the platform and the moving cable was carrying us steeply up above the tree-tops into a world of silence and absolute privacy.

I smiled at her. A fifteen-minute *tête-à-tête* in mid-air was something I hadn't reckoned on, but the prospect was pleasantly stimulating and I was quite prepared to cope.

" Nice of you to have me," I said.

" Not at all."

" Let's hope we get on all right. It's a bit late to scream now! "

The girl looked amused.

" Perhaps we'd better introduce ourselves. My name's James Renison."

" Mine's Carol Harvey. Hallo again! "

There was a little pause. Then I said, " Are you on holiday? "

" In a way. I've been visiting a friend in Boppard."

I glanced involuntarily at the hand that rested on the chair arm a few inches from my own. There was no ring.

" A girl friend," she told me, with a smile. " Ilsa said I positively must see the view from the top before I left and she couldn't come herself because the baby's teething, so I came alone. . . . What are *you* doing here? "

" Oh, just passing through. I've been in Zermatt—ski-ing."

" I guessed you'd been in the mountains—you're so brown. Was it fun? "

"Yes, we had a splendid ten days. The snow was perfect. Unfortunately the man I was with was called back suddenly and had to catch a plane. So I'm driving myself home by easy stages."

"I noticed the G.B. plate on your car," Carol said. It was as though she were excusing herself for having been forward.

We were high up over the hillside now. The wooded slope below us had become rugged and very steep. The only sign of life, apart from the couples suspended ahead and behind us, was a party of rucksacked figures toiling up a zigzag path. The silence was complete.

"You know," Carol said, "I'd love to bring a book up here in the summer and just travel up and down in a chair all day."

"It's a nice thought," I agreed. I was very conscious of her closeness. I could almost count her eyelashes, which were dark and very long.

The expanding view below was worth attention, too, and for a while we concentrated on it. The riverside town had become a collection of dots in a setting of vineyards. The broad Rhine had narrowed to a streak of quicksilver.

"It all looks much better from up here, doesn't it?" Carol said.

"Don't you like Boppard?"

"I think the town's quite attractive, but it's so terribly noisy—all those cars and trains, and the barges pounding up and down day and night. And—well, it does all look a bit grey and dusty, don't you think?"

"They haven't really got over the war," I said. "I'm always astonished when I hear people at home talking enviously about Germany's recovery. They've done a

terrific amount, of course, but the place still looks bat-
tered after fifteen years. I've been over a lot of it, and
it's the same story almost everywhere."

" Do you travel much? "

" A great deal, yes. Most of it's official, though—
conferences and things. I work at the Foreign Office."

" Do you! You must be very clever."

I smiled. " I'm afraid that doesn't follow."

" Will you be an ambassador one day? "

" More likely an attaché on the moon, the way things
are going."

" You'll need a big space suit," Carol said.

We were coming up now to the top platform. As the
chair swung over the concrete strip I showed her how to
undo the bar in front of her and we scrambled out. I was
prepared for her to go off on her own now that we'd
reached the top, but she showed no sign of wanting to.
There was a restaurant to the right, and beside it a path
signposted " *Aussichspunkt*," which we took. The air was
cooler here because of the height, but it was still very
pleasant. The fragrance of pines was all around us; the
first spring flowers were showing beside the path. Sounds
of laughter came from the woods. The atmosphere was
heady.

A short stroll through the trees brought us to the cele-
brated viewpoint and we joined the crowd there, gazing
down at the spectacular panorama. Deep in the valley,
it was possible to make out four separate reaches of the
winding Rhine, all apparently disconnected. Exclama-
tions of " *Schön!* " and " *Wunderbar!* " exploded around us.

" It *is* rather breathtaking," Carol said. " I'm so glad
I came."

" Me too."

" But you're not looking at it! "

" No," I said.

She gave a little laugh.

We lingered for a while, and then I suggested we should walk back to the restaurant for a glass of hock on the terrace. Sitting opposite her, I had a chance to examine in more detail her quite remarkable good looks. It was her expression, I decided, that was so attractive —there was a kind of mischievous inscrutability about it, a tantalising hint of secret depths. Everything about her contributed to the effect—the high cheek bones, the delicately arched brows, the dark, quizzical eyes, the provocative upward tilt at the corners of her mouth, the slightly stubborn chin, even the nonchalant set of her hair. She was, I guessed, no more than twenty-five, but she had the poise and assurance of a much older woman. Her impeccable grooming suggested an almost professional care for her appearance. If she'd been taller, I'd have thought she might be a model.

We sat talking for quite a while. Our conversation was lightly exploratory, the stuff of first acquaintance. I told her a little more about my holiday, enthusing over the Matterhorn; and about my companion, Tom Winslow, who was an up-and-coming physicist; and about my own work in London. Carol asked me where I lived, and I told her about my service flat overlooking St. James's Park.

" A pampered bachelor? " she said, with a teasing smile.

" I'm afraid so."

" It sounds very grand. I live in London, too—but I look after myself."

" What do you do in London? "

" I'm in show business."

I said, " Ah! " Much was explained. " What sort of show? "

" Oh, mostly variety—song and dance routines, and little sketches—that sort of thing. . . . It's a bit precarious, but television has helped."

" Pity—I don't often get a chance to look," I said. " Too many memoranda to write. . . . I've obviously been missing something."

" I wouldn't say so. . . . Then I tour a good deal—at least, I used to. That's how I met Ilsa."

" You mean you were appearing in Boppard? "

" No, but in some of the bigger towns—Coblenz— Mainz. . . . It was three years ago. Ilsa was in the same bill, and we kept in touch afterwards."

" Are you doing anything at the moment? "

" No, I'm what we call ' resting '—which means no bookings, in case you don't know. . . . So it seemed a good chance to come and see her." Carol looked at her watch. " You know, I'll have to be going. . . ."

I got up reluctantly, and together we walked back to the *sesselbahn*. We talked less on the way down. I don't know what she was thinking about, but I was thinking about her. At the bottom of the chair lift I suggested I should drive her to her friend's house, and she accepted gratefully. Five minutes later we pulled up outside a narrow, ancient house in a back street.

" That was a nice ride," Carol said. " Thank you. . . . It's been a most pleasant morning."

" Perhaps we could meet again in London," I said. " When are you going back? "

" The day after to-morrow. . . ."

" May I telephone you? "

" Why, yes, if you want to—I'd like it very much."
She told me her number, and I wrote it down. " It's not
my private phone," she said, " but someone will take a
message. . . . Well—*auf wiedersehen!* " She gave a little
smile, and went into the house.

CHAPTER II

MY THOUGHTS turned repeatedly to Carol on the way
home. It wasn't by any means the first time I'd been
suddenly attracted to a pretty girl, but in Carol's case it
was personality as much as looks that had made such a
deep impression on me, and I could hardly wait to see her
again. As it happened, I had to wait longer than I'd
expected, for the car gave unaccustomed trouble in the
Eifel and I was delayed two days. Then, when I rang
her Bayswater number on the evening of my return, I was
told by her landlady that she'd gone to Norfolk to visit
her married sister. It was almost a week after Boppard
before I was able to make contact with her. She sounded
pleased that I'd called her, asked about my journey, and
readily accepted an invitation to dine with me the
following day at a small but epicurean restaurant in
Soho.

I felt nervous as well as excited as I sat waiting for her
next evening at my favourite corner table. We had known
each other, I reminded myself, for just two hours in all,
on a magical spring day in highly romantic surroundings.
Now we were in a cold, grey London, a place of agents'
offices and in-trays! It would be awful if, at a second
meeting, Carol found me dull and unattractive. Or if

I discovered that I'd been cherishing a too-glowing image of her. But as soon as she appeared, and smiled, I stopped worrying. She was so obviously glad to see me again—and she was quite as lovely as I'd remembered. The boyish hair-do had turned into a sophisticated coiffure, and in a turquoise dress that framed her gleaming shoulders she looked enchanting. As we sipped our apéritifs and light-heartedly exchanged our bits of news, I could hardly believe in the good fortune that had brought us together.

Everything about the dinner was a success. Carol showed a healthy interest in the menu and we settled for avocado with a French dressing, Scotch salmon, and a soufflé that I knew would be superb. The wine we drank was Niersteiner—" for old Rhine's sake! " I said, with a silly grin. We chatted happily, easily, our eyes constantly meeting.

It was still quite early on in the meal when I asked her about her Norfolk trip. " Where does your sister live? " I inquired.

" It's on the north coast—a place called Embery Staithe," Carol told me. " Fay and her husband have a house on a creek there."

" That sounds fun. . . . Is your sister older or younger than you? "

" Neither," Carol said, with a smile. " We're twins."

" You don't say . . . ! Is she at all like you? "

" Very," Carol said. " We're identical twins, you see."

I stared at her. " You mean—you're *really* identical? "

" Yes."

" I can hardly believe it."

" Why not? "

" Well, if you really want to know I wouldn't have thought the miracle could be repeated."

Carol laughed out loud. " It's not an uncommon thing, you know."

" But—surely you're not *exactly* alike? "

" We are. The only difference anyone has ever been able to discover is that Fay has a tiny mole on one ear, and I haven't."

" It's fascinating! " I said. " You know, I don't think I've ever talked to an identical twin before. . . . Are you alike in disposition too? "

" Almost completely. Fay's a bit bossier, but that's only because she ate more when she was a baby and got used to pushing me around. We've the same tastes, the same outlook—everything."

I still found it difficult to take in. " Do you like it? " I asked. " Being a twin? "

" I don't dislike it. It's great fun when you're small, of course, because you've always got someone of your own age to play with, and even when you're grown up it's nice to feel you've got one certain friend and ally in the world."

I said, " I'm rather surprised you didn't mention it at Boppard. It must be about the most important thing in your life, so far."

" It is, of course," Carol agreed. She smiled. " But one doesn't necessarily want to present oneself at a first meeting as being—well, exactly like someone else."

" No—I can see that . . ."

" Actually, Fay and I get on wonderfully together, and always have—but some identical twins resent the whole thing terribly. They can even hate each other."

" Because they feel they're not unique? "

" Well, there can be all sorts of psychological compli-cations—but that's partly it. They feel they've had only half an endowment."

" But you don't feel that? "

" Not in the least. You see, although Fay and I were brought up together and went to the same school and so on, we were always treated as quite separate person-alities. For one thing, Mother didn't much like the idea of identical twins—she felt it was too much like having a litter, which was rather absurd—so she always wanted us to appear as different as possible. But mainly it was Daddy—he was a tremendous individualist himself and he decided right from the beginning that he wasn't going to have us grow up as a unit. He didn't actually try to keep us apart and I'm sure that was wise, it would have been overdoing it, but he used to get awfully mad if people cooed over us just because we were alike. He said we were human beings, not playthings, and right from the start we were dressed differently and given different toys and put to bed in different rooms. . . ."

" Didn't you mind? "

" Not more than any other young children, I don't think. Twins can be trained and disciplined like anyone else—they accept what they're used to. Anyway, it didn't seem to have any bad effect on Fay and me, and though we couldn't feel closer to each other than we do, we're certainly two complete people."

" Your father sounds rather sensible," I said.

" Well, in that way he was, at any rate. . . . He's dead now. He died when we were sixteen."

" I'm sorry. . . . What about your mother? "

" She married again—a Brazilian. She's living in Rio."

I nodded slowly. There was a little pause while the waiter cleared away some of the debris. Then I said, " So you went into show business. And what did Fay do? "

Carol smiled. " I'm afraid she did the same thing. Daddy wouldn't have approved at all, but really he was responsible—he was an actor himself, quite a good one, so I suppose it was in the blood. We weren't either of us brilliant, but we did have talent. In any case we were very hard up and it was the easiest way for Fay and me to make a living—if you're identical twins on the variety stage it's half the battle. So we became a professional team and went around together everywhere, singing and dancing. We had a thought-reading act, too, that used to go over rather well."

" Real thought-reading? "

" Oh, no, it was just a trick, but because we were twins people were convinced it was telepathy."

" *Can* identical twins read each other's minds? "

" Not in that sort of way—at least, I don't think so. There's the famous story, of course, of the twins at school who studied half the text-books each and answered the whole examination paper—but I've never believed it. . . . What there is is a sort of co-ordination—which is hardly surprising considering the minds of identical twins are as much alike as their faces. Fay and I quite often find ourselves making exactly the same remark, or the same response to a question, at exactly the same moment— though that kind of thing happens to other people as well. We do sometimes find that we get uneasy about each other when we're apart, and discover afterwards that there's been some illness or trouble."

" I suppose that could be a sort of thought-reading," I said. " A very close rapport, anyway. . . ." I poured a little more wine. " Tell me, when did your sister marry? "

" It was last November—four months ago."

" Do you visit her often? "

" Fairly often. I don't like to overdo it, though. I wouldn't want Arthur to feel he'd got a troupe on his hands! "

I laughed. " I should think Fay's marriage must have changed your life quite a bit? "

" Oh, it has," Carol said. " I've missed her enormously, and I know she's missed me. But we agreed long ago that it would be wrong for us to try and stick together if one of us wanted to marry—so when the time came we just took the separation as philosophically as we could."

" And you went on with your job? "

" As well as I could. It was much more difficult to get bookings, of course, once the double act was broken up. In fact, I don't really know what I'd have done, but Arthur helped me—he's been terribly generous. He said it was he who'd split up the partnership, so it was only fair that he should pay compensation. I wouldn't have been able to go to Germany except for him. I feel rather awful about it, but he's very rich so it isn't as bad as it might be—and I *am* hoping to make a niche for myself in time."

" You will," I said—though I wasn't really thinking about her career at that moment. I was too intrigued by the situation she'd disclosed. " One thing puzzles me— if you and Fay are so much alike, and you've always been together, what made Arthur go for Fay rather than for you? "

" Oh, that's easy. . . . We'd been playing in Norwich,

and at the end of one of the dances Fay slipped and hurt
her leg. She had to go to Norwich Hospital to do occu-
pation therapy—treadling a machine, actually—and
Arthur Ramsden was there, too. He'd splintered a bone
in his finger while he was sailing, and he was working a
printing machine next to her. So they treadled, and
printed, and got to know each other—and that was
that."

I said, " What would have happened if you'd gone
along and made the tea? "

Carol laughed. " Ah, that's something we'll never
know! "

" Anyway, what sort of man is Arthur? "

" He's good looking—a bit temperamental—rather a
complex character, I'd say. I don't really know him very
well yet. He can be very charming—I can quite see why
Fay fell for him. . . . He's a lot older than she is—about
forty."

" He left it late."

" Well, it isn't his first marriage. He had a frightful
experience the first time—he married someone when he
was in his twenties and she was drowned on the honeymoon."

" I say—what an absolutely appalling thing! "

" Wasn't it? He's not really been very lucky since,
either—he developed diabetes very badly a few years
ago and now he has to have enormous quantities of
insulin."

" It sounds as though your sister has taken on quite
a lot."

" Yes—though not as much as you'd think. Arthur
leads a completely normal life, as far as I can see. He's
got heaps of interests, and he's very active—sails a lot,

B

walks, watches birds. They both seem to have a very good time."

" Will he get any worse? "

" Apparently not—he's about as bad as he can be. Stabilised, I think they call it."

" Can they have a family? "

" His doctor says there's no reason why they shouldn't —and I know Fay would like to."

" Perhaps *they'll* have identical twins, too! "

" Oh, that's not a bit likely—and I certainly wouldn't want them to. Identical twins are often a frightful trouble to have and to bring up, you know. I don't really think they're very desirable at all."

I said, " I know one who is! "

Carol smiled. " May I have some more coffee, please? "

We continued to talk till the restaurant emptied and the waiter began to hover. Then I drove Carol back to her lodging in Bayswater. She'd clearly taken only limited advantage of Arthur's generosity, for the district was decayed and the large house Victorian and ugly. She had a furnished room on the second floor, she told me, with a kitchenette and use of bath. She didn't ask me in, and I didn't want her to. All I was concerned about was when I could see her again. " To-morrow? " I said eagerly. She shook her head, smiling—but when I pressed her she agreed to meet me the day after. It had been a wonderful evening, she said—she'd enjoyed every minute of it. The scent of her filled the car. I put my arm round her and kissed her. The kiss became much more than a good night salute, and she was trembling a little when she released herself. " Good night, James,"

she said softly.   She slipped out of the car, and gave a
little wave, and went indoors.   I stayed, waiting for her
light to go on, and she waved again before she drew the
curtains.

I drove home in a state of crazy exhilaration.   It *had*
been a wonderful evening, in every way—full of surprises,
but all of them nice ones.   Carol could so easily have
turned out to be madly attractive and nothing else—but
I knew now that she was highly intelligent as well.   There
was certainly no question in her case of half an endowment—she seemed to me to have everything.   Insight,
common sense, courage—and a proud independence.
She'd been a delight to talk to—and we'd got on mar-
vellously.   She *must* like me quite a lot, I told myself, or
she'd never have agreed to see me again so soon.   As
for me, I was quite simply head over heels in love with her.

CHAPTER III

THINGS MOVED as fast after that as my duties in an over-
worked Department of the F.O. would allow.   There was
a Foreign Ministers' conference in the offing, intended to
prepare the way for an eventual Summit meeting, and
my chief, John Allenby, was taking masses of work home
with him every night and returning to the office a little
paler each morning.   However, I couldn't persuade
myself that this was the moment for total self-sacrifice on
my part.   My eyes were now on a summit of my own,
which I felt would prove a lot more fruitful than the
forthcoming one with Mr. K.   Very soon I was deep in

a whirlwind courtship, seeing Carol every day, dining and dancing whenever I could snatch a clear evening, shuttling between St. James's and Bayswater after late-coffee sessions, and at week-ends driving out into the country. It was a period of exciting discovery, and rapturous happiness. I was quite sure of my own feelings, and I had little doubt about Carol's as the days went by. I hadn't spoken yet of marriage—I didn't want her to feel she was being rushed—but I knew I wanted to marry her, and as soon as possible. From my point of view, there was no reason for delay. I was thirty, I was well embarked on a career, and thanks to a whacking inheritance from my paternal grandmother I was extremely well off and in a position of absolute independence. There were no obstacles.

At an early stage I told Carol I'd very much like it if she'd come down and meet my people, who lived in the family house at Melwood on the Ashdown Forest, and she said she'd love to. I rang Mother, who said, " Of course, James—we'll be delighted. Bring her to lunch on Saturday." Mother sounded very calm about it. She asked me who Carol was, and I told her we'd met in Germany and that she was an actress, and Mother said, " Really, dear?—that sounds very exciting," in a tone which made it quite clear that she wasn't taking me seriously. I couldn't altogether blame her. The romances I'd had in the past had all fizzled out before they'd got properly started—through sheer bad picking on my part, Mother had thought, characteristically refusing to believe there could be anything lacking in me except judgment. In her view I was much too susceptible to outward appearances, too easily taken in by vivacity and prettiness—and on the record her view was understandable. At times I probably *had* been impetuous. However, that was all over now. . . .

Carol was unusually quiet when we drove down to Sussex on the Saturday and I guessed she was beginning to have cold feet about the visit. She'd naturally asked me quite early about my parents and I'd told her, in as casual a way as possible, that my father had been Governor of one of our vestigial colonies until his retirement, that he'd been given the usual knighthood, and that he was now being a country gentleman and writing his memoirs. She'd taken all that in her stride—at least, I'd thought so—but the sight of the imposing house, and the park, and the ornamental lake, seemed to unnerve her. " Darling, I'm scared," she said, as I drew up in front of the porticoed entrance. " This isn't my world at all."

" It won't be anyone's much longer, except the National Trust's," I told her. " It's certainly not mine —you know that. Anyway, it doesn't mean a thing. Don't worry—you look absolutely divine! "

In fact, everything went off very well indeed. Father was quite Edwardian in his attentions, and made no attempt to conceal his admiration. Mother—who very quickly sensed that this time I meant business—inserted her searching little questions into the conversation with adroitness and tact. Both parents were as intrigued as I had been to learn that Carol was an identical twin, and the talk covered some familiar ground. Carol, whose stage fright had now left her, was composed and cool. I felt proud of her.

Late that evening, when I'd returned to my flat after

taking Carol home, Mother rang up. I'd rather expected
that she would. " So—what do you think of her? "
I asked.

" Well, dear, she's charming and intelligent and very,
very lovely. . . ."

That sounded fine, but I sensed reservations. " I'm
glad you think so," I said, " because I'm hoping to
marry her."

" Yes—we rather had that impression! "

" Of course, I don't know for certain that she'll have
me—I haven't asked her yet."

" Oh, she'll have you, dear. . . ." There was a little
pause. " You don't think perhaps you're rushing things
a bit, do you? After all, you've only known her for a
week or two—it's a very short time."

" I feel quite sure about her," I said.

" As long as it's not just an infatuation. . . ."

" It's not," I said firmly.

" Well—I must say I'd have felt happier if you'd
known a little more about her background. Her mother
seems to have behaved in a very peculiar way, going off
like that—and Carol doesn't appear to have any other
family at all."

" She has a very delightful sister," I said.

" I thought you hadn't met her."

" I haven't—but she's exactly like Carol—remember? "

Mother laughed. " Well, you've obviously made up
your mind, so there's no more to be said. And I suppose
it is time you settled down. . . . You'll let us know your
plans, won't you? "

" Of course."

There was another little pause. Then Mother said,

" We *did* like her, dear—and we hope you'll both be very happy. . . ."

I lunched with Carol on the following day and afterwards, walking in the park, I asked her to marry me. She said she would. That evening I managed to get away from the office early and we went along to Aspreys and chose a solitaire diamond for her ring.

CHAPTER IV

I WAS eager now to meet Carol's sister—partly from curiosity about the other half of the " miracle," but also because I was keen to observe the twins together. I couldn't imagine any serious problems arising for me out of their relationship, but the sort of affinity they had was obviously something that would have to be reckoned with in a marriage. Carol had already rung Fay and told her the news of her engagement, and presently an invitation came asking us to go and spend a week-end in Norfolk.

On the following Saturday, a lovely April day, we drove up in the Lagonda to Embery Staithe—a comfortable three-hour run from town. I was already in the mood to like everything I saw, and I found the little village quite enchanting. It was actually in two parts. There was a cluster of houses on the main road, with a shop, and a pub, and one of those impressive churches that the medieval wool merchants built in that part of the world, and a lot of trees. Then, well away from the road, there was a very picturesque waterfront, with a dozen old cottages, a boatyard full of dinghies, a small but superior-looking hotel, and the Ramsdens' house, all ranged round the arc of a quiet and unspoilt tidal creek. The hotel was at one end of the arc; the Ramsdens' house, a hundred yards distant, at the other. The house—modern, but beautifully designed and constructed of mellow old brick—was a delight to the eye. It stood right on the edge of the creek, rising behind the grassed-over sea wall that kept the high tide within bounds. I parked the Lagonda beside Arthur's Daimler and we walked along a tamarisk-lined path to the open front door.

I had a moment of slight trepidation as I followed Carol inside and heard Fay's step. It would be disconcerting, to say the least, if the twins proved to be so much alike that I had difficulty in distinguishing between them. To me, whatever she said, Carol *was* unique, and I didn't want her duplicated. But as Fay greeted me, I saw that I need have no anxiety on that score. It was as though she had made a conscious effort to be different. Her dark hair had a faint, artificial touch of gold, and she wore it longer than Carol. Her clothes had a robust country look. Her lipstick toned with the deep wind-tan she had got from a winter on the bleak East Anglian coast. But the thing which most differentiated her from Carol —an obvious one that I hadn't thought of—was her attitude to me. Fay was friendly and detached—much as Carol had been during our first meeting at Boppard. Carol was in love with me, and showed it in every glance. Merely by her relationship to me, she would remain unique.

All the same, the likeness in physical detail was fascinating. Feature by feature, all Carol's beauty was exactly reproduced in Fay. Looking from one to the other of them, I saw the same dark eyes, set in precisely the same enigmatic way; the same well-marked eyebrows and eyelashes, exact to a hair; the same contours of cheek and chin; the same mischievously curving mouths. Their voices, too, were identical. When Fay said " Hallo " to me, it could just as well have been Carol by the car at Boppard. Even their gestures were alike—the artless-seeming but carefully studied gestures that went with their profession. Made up and dressed to look alike, they would certainly have been indistinguishable to a stranger.

" Well," Fay said, smiling at me, " now that you've got over the first shock, let me take you upstairs. Arthur won't be long—he's bailing out the dinghy. . . . You're in your usual room, Carol, and we've put James in the front. . . . You don't mind my calling you James, do you? "

" I'd be very hurt if you didn't," I said.

" I feel I know you quite well already—Carol's talked so much about you on the telephone."

" That's quite enough of that! " Carol said.

Alone in my room I washed and unpacked and then stood by the open windows for a moment, gazing out in deep contentment. The view had the peculiar, soothing charm of the East Anglian flats. To the right, the sea wall stretched away, curving and twisting, till it lost itself in a distant line of sand dunes. On the landward side of the wall were lush meadows and grazing cattle, the fields divided by dikes and drains. On the water side there was the winding main channel, sparkling in the sun. Ahead and to the left, as far as the eye could see, there were bare saltings, cut by innumerable rills and creeks. The channel seemed to turn away from the sea wall at the foot of the dunes and run parallel with them for a while. Where the dunes ended, there was a flash of blue—the exit to the sea, a mile or so away. In all my field of vision there wasn't a habitation or any human figure. It wouldn't have been everyone's idea of a good place to live, but—on this warm April day, at least—I thought it perfection.

Presently I went downstairs, passing in the hall a chubby, fresh-faced girl of seventeen or so who said, " Good morning, sir," with a strong country accent. Evidently the maid. It was already clear that the Ramsdens believed in living comfortably. And tastefully, too. Thought as well as money had been lavished on the interior of the house. The décor was impeccable, the furniture choice. There were several very fine pictures on the walls. In the drawing-room there was a display cabinet of exquisite Meissen. I thought, a little wryly, of Carol's shabby lodging in Bayswater, and longed for the moment when I could take her out of it and give her a background that was worthy of her.

In a few moments Arthur came quietly in. He kissed Carol on the cheek, shook hands with me, and said the right things about our engagement. Because he was Fay's choice as a husband I studied him with more than ordinary interest. He was a tall, spare man with a sensitive face rather deeply lined for forty, and very pale blue eyes. He was, as Carol had said, quite good looking, but his expression in repose struck me as a bit strained. His welcome to me, for all his congratulations, seemed to lack heartiness, and I wondered for an uncomfortable moment if it was only Fay who was glad we had come.

The feeling passed during lunch. Once the talk was under way Arthur proved quite amiable. Perhaps, I thought, he was a shy man, whose reserve took a little breaking down. In any case, the girls made up for him. They were very gay, and obviously happy to be together again. There was a good deal of teasing to start with, and then we began to talk about the life in Norfolk, which Fay said she had found full and stimulating even in the winter, and a very welcome change from the rigours of professional touring. It seemed that she and Arthur were both ardent small-boat sailors and spent a lot of time on the water. Arthur, Fay told us, was particularly expert, and had won the Open Handicap for dinghies at the local regatta the previous August in a howling gale. " He had the prettiest girl on the creek to crew for him," she said, and added with a smile, " It was before my time, of course! "

Arthur smiled too, faintly. He had been watching Fay all the while she had been talking. It was a thing I was to notice often during that week-end—the almost hungry way in which his eyes dwelt on her.

As we got up from the table I made some admiring remark about the china in the cabinet and Arthur asked me if I'd like to see the rest of his treasures. It seemed he was an enthusiastic collector both of china and pictures and spent a good deal of time in sale rooms. He took me on a leisurely tour of the house, pointing out with rather charming diffidence the finer pieces in his collection. Then we had coffee, and afterwards we all went for a stroll along the sea wall. It was an ideal place for walking, Fay said, because in addition to the path along the top there were also well-marked tracks at ground level on each side of it, which meant there was usually shelter whichever way the wind was blowing. I could imagine that in winter that would be quite a point.

Arthur dropped back with me after a time, letting the girls go on ahead. A little silence followed. I didn't break it, because I could see he was on the verge of saying something, though he seemed to be having difficulty in getting started. I learned afterwards that his speech was sometimes affected by a slight impediment. When the words finally came out, they were unexceptionable.

" I'm really delighted," he said, " that you and Carol are going to marry—and I do congratulate you most warmly. . . . It isn't often that one man can tell another with absolute certainty that his prospective wife will turn out a winner, but I happen to be in that position. To know Fay is to know Carol—and they're both wonderful."

I nodded. I needed no convincing, but it was pleasant to hear him say so.

" Meeting Fay," Arthur went on, " was the greatest piece of good fortune I ever had. It changed my life completely. I was pretty lonely before that—I don't make friends easily, and I've only one rather distant relation that I know of. In fact, I was a very crotchety person! " He smiled his wintry smile. " But Fay took me on, and she's coped—and it's been a wonderful five months. . . . She means everything to me."

" I can well believe it," I said. If Arthur was in the mood for confidences, I was quite happy to co-operate.

" They're remarkable girls—all the more amazing when you think of their background. Has Carol told you about it? "

" She's told me a little about her father and mother. Not a great deal."

" Well, the girls had a pretty rough passage, you know. From what I've been able to gather, their father had

stacks of personality and talent, but he was hopelessly
unreliable. Artistic temperament to the nth degree!
When he'd had a run of luck and was in the money he'd
heap luxuries on the family, take them travelling, all that
sort of thing—and when he hadn't they practically
starved. It was a life of extremes—they never knew
where they were. The fact that he drank like a fish didn't
help, either. It was drink that finished him off."

" I didn't know that," I said.

" Well, it's not a thing that Carol would fall over
herself to tell you. Fay didn't tell me till after we were
married, and I can't say I blame her. . . . Their mother
doesn't seem to have been much good, either. Very
attractive, I gather, but completely selfish and pleasure
loving—and the occasional bouts of luxury she enjoyed
no doubt gave her a taste for it. She virtually abandoned
them when they were seventeen—just went off with her
rich Brazilian and left them to shift for themselves."

" Yes, I know about her," I said. " I understand she
hasn't written to them much, either."

" Hardly at all—she's been a dead loss. There's no
doubt she just didn't like them—Carol's probably told
you, she had an almost pathological aversion to the idea
of identical twins—and she seized the first opportunity to
cut adrift and start a new life without them. The girls
felt it pretty keenly at first, I know, but of course they've
come to accept it. It's not a pleasant story. . . ." He
paused. " I only brought this up, James, because—well,
we're going to have more in common than most brothers-
in-law, and you'd be bound to hear all about it sooner or
later. I thought you might like to be assured by someone
who really knows the twins that they've inherited only the
good points from their rather unsatisfactory parents.

Personality, intelligence, and looks! So you don't have to worry on that score."

"It's nice of you to tell me," I said. "Not," I added with a smile, "that I'd have worried much, anyway. . . . I'm afraid I'm much too far gone!"

"I understand," Arthur said. "I was just the same myself—and after all, most of us have some pretty odd forebears not far back. . . . Skeletons in the cupboard! Well, I'm sure it's all going to be very satisfactory. I hear you're in the Foreign Office."

"I am."

"I'm sure you'll do well. If I may say so, you look just the type. Are you fixed up all right financially?"

"I was born with a silver spoon, I'm afraid."

"Well, there's no harm in that, if you don't let it spoil you. I was, too, in a way. . . . You'll forgive me for talking to you a little as though I were Carol's father, won't you?—she hasn't got anyone else to do the job."

"I don't mind in the least."

"I'm so glad she'll have security at last—she deserves it. She's had a very hard time these past months, and though we've tried to help her, she's been reluctant to accept anything substantial. . . . Well, that's that." Arthur looked as though he had satisfactorily discharged a duty. I rather liked him for having made the effort.

CHAPTER V

THAT EVENING we had quite a celebration. Fay had prepared a delightful meal with the help of Maureen, the little maid; and Arthur—who for no reason that I could see had become morosely preoccupied after our walk—cheered up and opened a bottle of excellent claret. He took only a token sip himself, I noticed, but he ate more or less the same as everyone else. His diabetes certainly didn't obtrude. The girls were in high spirits and kept dropping into bits of old " routines " for our amusement. I still found myself watching them in fascination and marvelling at the similarity even of their expressions. I no longer felt the least trace of anxiety about their twinship. There was no tendency to exclusiveness in their close relationship, and Fay seemed as whole-heartedly devoted to Arthur as any wife could be. Everything I saw of her strengthened—if that were possible—my feelings about Carol.

As the meal ended, Arthur said he'd like to take some photographs of us at the table—" the first for the Renison family album," he said with a dry smile—and he went off to get his camera. Photography, it seemed was another of his special interests. Using flashbulbs, he first took one of Carol and me together, and then one of me sitting between the twins. Afterwards he sat down with me and Carol, and Fay took a picture, manipulating the flash bulb with practised skill. Arthur had brought down some of the photographs he'd taken around the creek and he showed them to us. They were outstandingly good, particularly some telescopic studies of sea-birds nesting and in flight. " There's a bird sanctuary out beyond the Point," he explained. " Ram's Head Island—a wonderful spot."

" If it's a nice day to-morrow," Fay said, " perhaps we'll be able to go out there."

It proved to be a glorious day, balmy as summer, and the household was already active when I woke at seven. Along the passage, I could hear a steady flow of chatter from the twins. Arthur, evidently an early riser, was pottering about at the edge of the creek, getting his dinghy ready. A flower-scented breeze wafted gently through my window. It felt good to be alive.

At breakfast it was decided that as there wasn't comfortable room for four in the ten-foot dinghy, Arthur and I would sail it to the Point while the girls walked round the sea wall. " You two can go off together after lunch if you want to canoodle," Fay said to Carol. I remembered that Carol had once called her a bit bossy. She had, I realised, just a shade more positiveness in her manner—or perhaps it was simply that she was the hostess, the organiser of the outing. It was such a perfect day, she said, that we really ought to swim—and in a trice, costumes and towels had been found for everyone. I helped Arthur carry the impedimenta down to the boat —rug, picnic basket and drinks, his precious camera, and a pair of binoculars. Fay called out, " Got your insulin, darling? " and Arthur slapped his side pocket, and nodded. The girls set off, taking the path behind the bank, and Arthur pushed the boat out. The creek was emptying and the tide was with us, but the wind would be heading us a little on the first leg.

" Would you care to take her? " Arthur asked.

" No, you carry on," I said. " The channel looks a bit tricky to me."

He nodded, and let the boat gather way, steering dexterously between the moored craft and eyeing the shoals ahead. He sailed with a sort of grim concentration, more as though it were a skill he took pride in than as if he were really enjoying it. I sat watching his expert movements and listening to the gurgle of the water under the stem. It was all incredibly peaceful. The surface of the creek was scarcely ruffled; the saltings looked lovely under the wide sky. Somewhere a lark was trilling high up. It all seemed a very long way from Geneva conferences and problems of disengagement in Europe!

" Is it always as quiet as this? " I asked, gazing around. Apart from one or two figures back on the hotel terrace, there didn't seem to be a soul anywhere.

" It very often is," Arthur told me. " We get quite a bit of sailing activity at week-ends and in the summer, and boats take visitors to the island in the high season when the tides are right—but in the off-seasons, and particularly in mid-week, there's rarely anyone."

" I suppose cars can't get to the Point? "

" No, thank heaven—that's what's saved it. People simply won't walk a yard if they can help it. Of course, we get the odd naturalist and birdwatcher hiking out from the hotel, but most of the people who stay there are out of breath before they reach our house! I'd say that out there by the Point is one of the loneliest places in the country."

" How long have you lived here, Arthur? "

" Just over five years. . . ." He was silent for a moment, watching his sail. " I used to farm, you know. . . . Then

c

I contracted diabetes, and I decided to take things more quietly. I knew this spot from my Cambridge days—I'd always liked it. So when I discovered the house was for sale I bought it. The odd thing is, ever since I came here I haven't seemed to have a moment to spare."

" That's a good sign," I said.

" Probably . . . I take quite an interest in parish pump politics—particularly questions of preservation and amenity. Then there's the Ornithological Society—sale rooms—photography. Nearly always with Fay, of course. . . . And I'm taken up quite a bit with this disease of mine."

" I suppose so."

" Oh, I don't mean I'm a hypochondriac—I don't actually worry about my health at all. I'm simply interested in the disease and its treatment—it's an absorbing study. I'm the hub of a sort of diabetic society in Norfolk. I write articles occasionally, and contribute quite substantially to national research. There's a good deal of work still to be done in the field."

" Have you any idea how you got it? "

" Not really. Its origins are a bit of a mystery, you know. Some people think there's a nervous element in it, but it's not proved. Obesity seems to have something to do with it—it's often called a disease of the sedentary rich. Actually I did get abnormally fat for a while, even though I was farming. You wouldn't think so now, would you? "

" Indeed I wouldn't. . . ." He hadn't an ounce of spare flesh on him. " So what happens—you have to take insulin all the time, do you? "

" Yes—a massive dose morning and evening. I inject it myself. It's very simple once you've got the hang of it. It means no more to me now than brushing my teeth."

" I noticed Fay asked you if you'd got the stuff. . . ."

" She always does when I go out. I'm absolutely dependent on it, you see. If I missed a dose I'd probably be in a coma in ten or twelve hours. I had a rather close shave once—got stuck in a car miles from anywhere, and no insulin—so now I carry it with me wherever I go, just in case."

" And as long as you have it regularly, you feel quite all right? "

" Absolutely fine. I can lead a full, energetic life, with no real privations at all. It's amazing, don't you think, considering that diabetes was a killer thirty years ago? "

" It certainly is. . . . Don't you even have to diet? "

" Oh, yes—though a layman would hardly spot it. The thing is, you have to maintain an artificial balance between your diet and your insulin. At first I used to have to weigh and measure my food, but now I've got it down to such a fine art I can take a look at a meal and know almost to a unit what insulin I'll need to balance it."

" So Fay doesn't really have to bother much? "

" Hardly at all. You see, by the time I met her I was an old hand and knew all about it—she didn't have to worry. The only trouble is, I'm a bit of an epicure—so she's always having to think up interesting new dishes. But she's very good about it—we really take the whole thing very much in our stride. . . ."

I said, " I think you've both shown a lot of courage."

His face became rather solemn. " Life's a struggle, isn't it? If you once give in, you've had it. . . ." He started to turn the dinghy in towards the shore as we approached the Point. " Well, this is where we land. . . ."

We hauled the boat out and dropped the sails. The girls had emerged from behind the sea wall but were still some distance away and Arthur suggested we should climb to the top of the sandbank so that I could look around. We negotiated the steeply rising beach and wound our way along a sandy path through the marram grass till we reached a viewpoint. On the other side of the bank, but quite a long way out now, lay the open sea, blue and quiet. To the left, beyond the Point, there was a deep channel some fifty yards wide where the creek poured out to join the sea, and across the channel there were more dunes.

" That's Ram's Head Island," Arthur said. " It's nearly two miles long, though you wouldn't think so, looking at it from here. It's a most interesting place—the sandhill formations are quite unusual. Fay and I spend a lot of time there in good weather."

" There's quite a current in the channel," I said, gazing down at the racing water.

" Yes, it really sluices on the ebb, doesn't it? Fay thinks nothing at all of swimming across—but I have to sail or row."

We walked on for a few yards. There was a notice board beside the path, and I paused to read it. It said: THE PUBLIC ARE WARNED TO RETURN FROM THE FAR SANDS BEFORE THE TIDE FLOWS.

" Sounds quite poetical," I said. " What do they mean by the Far Sands? "

Arthur pointed to the right, in the opposite direction from the island. The coast, I saw, curved round to form a wide, semi-circular bay, with what looked like a small town a couple of miles away on the other side of it. "When the tide's right out," Arthur said, " the whole bay becomes a wilderness of sand with a lot of complicated channels. It's a bit like a river delta. People go out at low water to dig for cockles or lugworms or just to explore, and if they don't watch the tide they can easily get cut off. There are several of these notices along the coast. . . . That's our local town, by the way—Fairhaven. . . ."

At that moment there was a hail from below—the girls had arrived, and were waving. We quickly joined them and brought the things up from the dinghy to a sheltered, sunny nook in the dunes. It was very warm out of the breeze and Fay suggested we should have our swim right away. We changed and went down to the creek, choosing a little inlet where the tide was slack. The water was bracingly cold, though not more so than on many a summer day. Arthur, it turned out, could barely swim at all, and kept close to the edge, splashing vigorously. " I never could get the knack of it," he told me, a little sheepishly, " and I'm afraid I'm too old to learn now." I thought he looked a bit blue.

It was an exhilarating swim for the rest of us, and we soon warmed up afterwards in the sun. Carol started to row around in the dinghy—she was a real water girl, like Fay, when she got the chance—and Arthur took some more photographs. Then he went and sat by himself on a little knoll, a few yards above us, with his glasses beside him and the old, preoccupied look on his face. He was certainly a queer bird. He rejoined us for lunch, and we had a pleasant picnic. When we'd finished, Carol said, " Come on, James, let's go and find the real sea—I want to see some waves," and we set off together towards the Far Sands and the distant streak of blue.

It felt marvellous to be on our own again. We didn't talk much at first—we just strolled along, arms round each other, blissfully content. Then, as the going became more difficult and we had to separate, Carol said, " Well —what do you think of Fay? "

" If I told you," I said, " it would only make you unbearably conceited! "

She laughed. " And Arthur? "

I hesitated. " Well, he's an interesting chap, and quite likeable—but——"

" But what? "

" Would you have fallen for him if you'd happened to meet him first? "

" Darling, that's a thing one can't possibly know. . . . I certainly can't imagine it now."

" Perhaps he appealed to Fay's maternal instinct," I said. " Meeting him in hospital, finding he was a diabetic, hearing about his tragic first marriage and so on. . . ."

Carol nodded. " I wouldn't be surprised if you were right. He is slightly pathetic, don't you think . . . ? "

" He's a good deal moodier than I expected from your description."

" I know," Carol said, frowning. " He seems to have struck a bad patch—I've never seen him quite like this before. Fay was talking about it as we walked round. She's a bit worried, actually."

" I'm not surprised. Hasn't she any idea what the trouble is? "

" Not a clue. Arthur swears there isn't any trouble— but he certainly behaves as though he's got something on his mind."

" He's cheerful enough when he's talking about his

diabetes," I said, " so it can't be that. . . . And about Fay, of course."

" I know—he's absolutely devoted to her, isn't he? And so is Fay to him."

We left it there and concentrated on our surroundings, which had become quite remarkable. By now we were half a mile or more from the shore, and the place we'd reached was unlike anything I'd ever seen before. We were wandering in a maze of channels, most of them dry at the moment, cut out to a great depth by the fierce ebb and flow of the streams. Beside the channels, the sand had been carved into tormented gargoyle shapes, with deep holes and steep mounds and treacherous soft patches in which we several times plunged to our knees. It was indeed a wilderness, and a very tiring one, and we soon gave up our idea of reaching the sea. Instead, we took a wide sweep back towards the dunes, skirting a deep stream with small black buoys along one side, that looked like the main channel into Fairhaven. We were both quite thankful when we reached smooth, firm ground again. If those were the Far Sands, I thought, they couldn't be too far for me!

As we approached the dunes, Carol suddenly returned to the earlier topic. " I do hope Fay and Arthur are going to be all right," she said. She'd evidently been dwelling.

I said, " Oh, I'm sure they will be."

" It's hard to be sure. Marriage is such a gamble."

I looked at her a little anxiously. " You're not getting cold feet, are you? "

" About us? " She smiled and shook her head. " No, darling—I wish you and I were married at this very moment."

CHAPTER VI

IN FACT, we were married just six weeks later. By Carol's choice, the wedding was held in the village church at Embery Staithe, the only place with which she felt she had any links. By her choice, too, the ceremony was quiet and simple—partly, I guessed, because she wanted to avoid a mass descent by the Renison family when she herself had no relatives to produce but Fay. I was entirely on her side, and the occasion turned out to be wholly enjoyable, imposing no nervous strain on anyone. Carol had some old theatre friends along, who were all squeezed for a night into Fay's house. Arthur gave the bride away. My parents came up, and a handpicked few of my relations, and Tom Winslow was my best man. Carol had written to her mother saying she was going to get married and had had a brief letter back wishing her every happiness, which I gathered was all that had happened in Fay's case. I couldn't help regretting what seemed to me a most unnatural lack of interest, but, as Arthur had said, the girls were accustomed to it, and it certainly didn't cloud the occasion as far as Carol was concerned. She positively glowed with happiness. After the ceremony we had a pleasant celebration in the hotel at Embery Staithe, and in the evening we drove back to London and stayed at the flat. Next day we flew to Florence for our honeymoon.

I'd met couples who, for one reason or another, didn't really enjoy their honeymoon—but I certainly had no complaint about ours. It was just about the nearest thing to heaven on earth that I could imagine. Everything was perfect—our rapture in each other, the aching loveliness of that wonderful city, the kindliness of all the people we met, the blue skies that smiled on us. I would always remember it as an idyll.

When we got back to London we started to look for a larger and more suitable flat. The fact that we hadn't to think about the cost ought to have simplified the problem, but Carol—not without encouragement from me—had rather set her heart on one with a balcony overlooking the park and they're not so easy to come by. In the end, though, we managed to find just what we wanted—a very elegant flat not far from my old one, with a view so open that it was almost like living in the country—and we took it on a long lease. I had to leave most of the furnishing arrangements to Carol because of pressure at the office, but it worked out very well. For one thing, it was the first time in her life she'd been in a position to buy virtually whatever she wanted without considering the cost, and she naturally enjoyed it. For another, she showed a definite talent for making her surroundings attractive—just as Fay had done in Arthur's house. Relieved of all serious chores by the excellent " daily " we found, she could devote herself with single-minded enthusiasm to the pleasures of home-building. Our tastes turned out to be very similar, and I had no fault to find with the end-product. When the last picture was hung we had my people along to dinner, and Carol played hostess with such grace and charm that even Mother seemed to approve. Whatever Carol might have said earlier about my social background not being " her world," she was adapting herself to a life of wealth and privilege with effortless ease, and was obviously thrilled

to bits by it all. Her pleasure at being able to wear nice
clothes and jewellery that weren't part of a theatrical
wardrobe was quite touching, and I fully shared it. If
she had any nostalgic yearnings for the stage, they
certainly didn't show!

To me, being married to Carol was a constant delight.
I was still in the stage of being ecstatically, uncritically in
love, and she seemed to me quite flawless. She was so
lovely that merely to look at her was a refreshment. My
only regret was that I couldn't spend enough time with
her—my evenings began late, and free week-ends couldn't
always be relied on. But when we were together, the
hours were full of excitement and interest. Carol, I discovered, had had only a very sketchy formal education,
but her mind was so active and agile that she had learned
more as she went along than most people managed to do
from years of steady schooling. Moreover, she had the
chameleon's gift of adapting herself to her surroundings—
or perhaps just the intelligent woman's gift of making her
husband's interests her own. If I had been a plumber,
I thought, she would soon have known all there was to
know about pipes; as it was, she eagerly read the foreign
pages of *The Times* and any documents I brought home
that she was allowed to see. I should have known by
now how remarkable a girl she was, but I still found
myself caught up in surprise on occasion by her mental
quickness. After two months of fairly close companionship, I still felt that I really knew very little about her.
Whether or not there were facets of her character that
I hadn't yet seen, I always had the feeling that there were
—the feeling of exciting discoveries still to be made, of
secrets still uncovered. I didn't mind. Full knowledge
was no doubt an essential part of perfect " loving," as

opposed to " being in love," but it would come. In the meantime, I found the possibility of uncharted depths rather stimulating.

In August I had to fly to Bonn with John Allenby for a few days, and of course I wasn't able to take Carol. We'd known that these separations were bound to occur from time to time, and we both accepted the parting philosophically. Carol, who had kept in touch with Fay during the busy summer but hadn't had a chance to see her, took the opportunity to go up to Norfolk while I was away.

She was back in time to meet me at London Airport on my return. The joy of reunion was exquisite. I told her what Stevenson had said—" absence is a good influence on love and keeps it bright and delicate "—but Carol said ours was bright enough anyway and didn't need any aids. She sat very close to me in the car. She had picked up a becoming tan in Norfolk, but I thought I saw fatigue in her face. I told her briefly about my trip, and then asked her how things were at Embery Staithe.

" Not very good, darling," she said, and paused. " It's Arthur . . . Fay's very worried about him."

" Oh, lord," I said. " What's happened? "

" Well, he's been behaving even more strangely than he did when we were there in the spring. You know we thought he was depressed and moody then—but now he seems to be worse. Not all the time, but every now and again. . . . And that's not all. He's become more solitary than he used to be—he's been going off on his own a great deal, Fay says, and brooding a lot. He's even taken to going off along the sea wall after dark—which isn't very sensible, with so many things you can fall over."

" It sounds crazy. . . . Hasn't Fay spoken to him about it? "

" She has, yes—and she's tried several times to find out what's wrong, but he only gets annoyed and says there isn't anything and that he wishes she wouldn't fuss. It just doesn't sound like them—I'm really terribly miserable about it. Nothing actually happened while I was there, but the atmosphere's so strained that apart from leaving Fay I was quite thankful to get away. Fay says they've almost quarrelled sometimes. . . . Anyway, she got so worried about these late night walks of his that she started to follow him, and one night last week she caught up with him and it seems he was kneeling in the sand, with his back to the creek, almost as though he were praying."

" Good heavens! " I ejaculated.

" It was right out near the Point—among a lot of old sea defence stuff and really not at all a safe place to be in the dark. . . . Well, Fay showed herself, of course, and asked him what on earth he was doing, and he was angry with her for having followed him and they had quite a row. In the end he went stalking off alone, and she started off back, and she hadn't gone far before she thought she heard someone else moving about—which must be almost unknown there at night. So now Fay wonders if Arthur was meeting someone."

I said, " You don't mean another woman? "

" Well, it seems almost impossible to believe in Arthur's case, I know—but he has been so secretive and strange . . ."

" Did Fay tell him she'd heard someone else? "

" She did, as a matter of fact, but Arthur said he knew nothing about it and certainly wasn't meeting anyone,

and that he was just resting in the sand before turning
back when she found him, and that's all there is to it. . . .
Honestly, I felt like tackling Arthur about it myself and
telling him he wasn't being fair to Fay and that if he
went on behaving in such an idiotic way he'd spoil everything between them, but Fay wouldn't let me mention
it—she said it would only make things worse, and that
they'd have to sort it out for themselves. . . . But really,
darling, they do seem to have got into rather a mess—and
I don't understand why."

" It's extraordinary," I said. I was silent for a moment,
trying to imagine Arthur, with his diabetes, and his
beautiful wife whom he'd only recently married and who
was so fond of him, having a clandestine affair with some
local girl in the sandhills—and my imagination boggled.
I remembered the way he'd spoken to me about Fay, his
unstinted admiration of her, his obvious dependence on
her, and it seemed quite outside the bounds of possibility
that he would even have looked at anyone else. " It
sounds to me as though he ought to see someone," I said.
" Take some advice."

" Well, he's constantly seeing his own doctor about his
general health—they're always in touch. And as far as
anything else is concerned, he simply denies that there's
anything wrong with him—he says he's always had an
urge to go off on his own at odd times, and that for a man
of his temperament there's nothing at all unusual about
it. . . . So what can you do? "

" If Fay can't do anything," I said, " it's certainly hard
to see how anyone else can. . . ." I could see that Carol
was deeply disturbed, and I offered the only bromide
I could think of. " I dare say it's only a temporary thing
—Arthur's obviously a bit unstable, but they'll probably

settle down all right in the end. Married people are
bound to have their ups and downs."

" *We* don't," Carol said.

I crossed my fingers on the steering wheel. " Darling,
don't *say* things like that. . . .   There's still plenty of
time! "

CHAPTER VII

A FEW DAYS later we had more evidence of the unsatisfactory state of affairs at Embery Staithe. During one of
her frequent talks with Carol on the telephone, Fay disclosed that Arthur had suggested it might be a good thing
for both of them if she came and stayed with us for a week
or two on her own. They'd been living in each other's
pockets too much, he'd said, and a short break might
give them a fresh start. Maureen could go home to her
people and he'd look after himself—he'd rather enjoy it.
Apparently he'd pressed Fay quite hard, and though she
hadn't liked the idea at all and had postponed any decision, she told Carol Arthur was so insistent that she
thought she probably would be coming later on—in fact,
she'd practically agreed. Naturally Carol said she could
come any time. However, things seemed to improve a
little after that and the subject was temporarily dropped.
Arthur was reported to be less tiresome, and there'd been
no more night walks or major crises. The trouble, whatever it was, seemed to be blowing over. Fay sounded
much less miserable, and Carol was correspondingly
relieved.

Then, on a bright Saturday in early October, just as

we were finishing lunch, Carol suddenly said she'd like to go up to Norfolk. She'd tried to ring Fay several times during the morning but there hadn't been any reply and now—for no special reason that I could see—she had become acutely worried. I teased her about her twin's sixth sense and said I didn't think we ought to go and plant ourselves on Fay and Arthur without an invitation or even a word to say we were coming, but Carol wouldn't be argued out of it. If there were any difficulty when we got there, she said, we could stay at the hotel. By three o'clock we were away in the Lagonda, and by half-past five we were driving into Embery Staithe.

There was a bleak, end-of-season look about the place, very different from the last time I'd seen it. Most of the boats had gone from the creek, the hotel terrace was deserted, and there wasn't a single car parked on the waterfront or a single walker within sight. The quietness of the house matched the surroundings—even Maureen didn't seem to be at home. Then Carol remembered she always had Saturdays off and went into Norwich to see her boy friend, which accounted for her. The house was locked up, but Carol knew where a key was kept hidden in case of emergency and we found it and let ourselves in. Everything was in perfect order inside. I thought Fay and Arthur might have gone out in the car and we looked in the garage—but the car was there. So too, we noticed, were the dinghy sails. But when we glanced over the sea wall we saw that the dinghy wasn't.

" They must have gone for a row," Carol said, frowning.

I nodded, gazing out over the creek. A flat, grey calm had followed the fine morning, and it looked like rain. Dusk would be falling very soon, so I couldn't believe they'd be long. We started to stroll round the sea wall

towards the Point, keeping our eyes open for them, but
we hadn't gone more than a few hundred yards when the
rain began and we turned back. We might just as well
wait in the house, we decided. Fay and Arthur would be
equipped for the weather, and we weren't.

Shortly after seven a key turned in the front door and
Maureen came in. She was very surprised to see us—and
equally surprised to see we were alone. We'd been wrong,
it seemed, in imagining that Fay and Arthur were out
together. Mr. Ramsden, Maureen said, had gone off in
the dinghy alone that morning. It had been a beautiful
day, but too calm for sailing, and he'd left very early so
that he could row out with the tide—before eight o'clock,
Maureen told us—taking his lunch with him. He'd
suggested that Mrs. Ramsden should go too, but she'd
said she'd got some shopping to do and some important
calls to make in Fairhaven and had decided not to.
Maureen had then caught a bus into Norwich, so that
was all she knew.

By now, I was beginning to share Carol's uneasiness—
but about Arthur, rather than Fay. It was getting dark
outside, and the rain was coming down hard. It was
fantastic that he should still be out, particularly as it was
almost dinner-time and he needed his meals regularly.
It was equally odd about Fay, who by now should have
had the meal ready. It looked as though she'd gone
farther afield than Fairhaven—but not by car. I couldn't
make head or tail of it.

We discussed the position anxiously. There didn't
seem much point in going to look for Arthur in the dark,
for we'd no idea where he'd gone. Ram's Head Island
was only one of his many haunts. Between the island and
the mainland there were miles of creeks and saltings

stretching along the coast. Sometimes he'd been known to row to the next village, four miles away, and leave the dinghy and come back by bus. Perhaps he'd do that to-night. . . .

We had a couple of drinks, and sat waiting—and worrying. We discussed all sorts of possibilities, but nothing really made sense. If Arthur had landed somewhere, and rung Fay, and Fay had joined him for a meal out, she'd have taken the car. In any case, one or other of them would surely have got in touch with Maureen by now. It was possible, of course, that Arthur had had some accident—that was in all our minds. With boats, you could easily have accidents. But that still didn't account for Fay.

By nine o'clock, Carol was so anxious that she rang up the police at Fairhaven and said she thought Arthur might have got into difficulties with his boat. They knew Arthur well, of course, and though I couldn't see what they could possibly do at that hour they said they'd send someone round. Just before ten a police car drew up outside the house and a Sergeant Laycock came in to see what it was all about. Carol and I had seen him around —he was a youngish, tall, alert-looking man, with the mark of further promotion on him—and he knew us, too. We told him the few facts we had, and he stood with a puzzled expression on his face, trying to work it out. He didn't have any more success than we'd had. There might be some quite simple explanation, he said—which was true—but he obviously couldn't think of one.

We were still turning over the possibilities when the phone rang. I felt sure it must be Fay or Arthur, and Carol had the same thought. She snatched up the receiver and said, " Yes?—hallo . . . ? "

D

A man's voice, low, but clearly audible through the room, said, " Fay!—*darling!*—how did it go? Did you manage it? "

Carol's expression changed to one of bewilderment. " This isn't Fay," she said, " it's her sister. Who . . . ? "

There was a click as the caller hung up.

Carol put the receiver down, her face pale. A moment of silence followed. Then Sergeant Laycock said in a too matter-of-fact tone, " Someone for Mrs. Ramsden? "

" Apparently," Carol said.

" Not *Mr.* Ramsden? "

She shook her head. " I've no idea who it was."

Laycock crossed to the phone and spoke to the operator. He didn't get anywhere with trying to trace the call. It had been a local one, dialled.

" Well," he said, looking a trifle embarrassed, " I'd better get back to the station. We'll do what we can— make a few inquiries along the coast. . . . You'll let us know if they come in, won't you? "

I said we would, and he left us.

I got some whisky, and gave Carol a shot, and had one myself. She needed it more than I did.

" He mistook me for Fay," she said, staring at me.

I nodded. " That's very easy."

" He called her ' darling '. . . ."

I shrugged. " That doesn't mean a thing in Fay's world—*you* know that. . . . Someone she knew in the theatre, probably."

" What did he mean—' did you manage it? ' Manage *what?* And why ring off in such a hurry? "

I shook my head. At that stage I couldn't imagine either where Fay was or what she'd been up to.

CHAPTER VIII

WE SAT UP until the early hours, hoping for another phone call that would explain everything, but nothing happened. The police, evidently, had had no luck with their inquiries. The steady beat of the rain outside was anything but reassuring. When, finally, we gave up the vigil and went to bed, we were both too worried to sleep.

Daylight came as a blessed relief. At least something could be done now. The rain was beginning to die out and the morning promised to be fine. I rang the police at Fairhaven and told them we still had no news, and they said they hadn't either, and that they proposed to organise a search party to work along the coast and look for the dinghy. I said we'd like to help and arranged with them that we would cover the stretch around the Point and the island. We managed to borrow a rowing boat from Joe Clancy, the owner of the boat yard, and about eleven we set off, leaving Maureen at the house to take any messages.

It was a stiff pull out of the creek against the tide. While I concentrated on the rowing, Carol examined every inch of the saltings through the binoculars. If the boat was anywhere around, its mast should show above the grass. But the whole place was as bare as a billiard-table. We kept going, and when we reached the Point we landed and climbed to the look-out near the notice board, scanning the coast in both directions. There was no sign of the dinghy anywhere along the bay or on the side of the island that faced us.

We returned to the creek and rowed across the channel
to continue the search along the shore that was hidden
from us. I hauled the boat out and pushed the anchor
into the sand, while Carol gazed anxiously around.
Suddenly she cried, " What's that? " pointing to a dark
streak up on the tide mark about fifty yards away. I said,
" It's only a bit of wood, isn't it . . . ? " but we went over
to see.

It wasn't a bit of wood. It was an oar!

" It's one of Arthur's," Carol said, in a shaky voice.
" It's been washed up. . . . Oh, James! "

I tried to soothe her. I pointed out that even if, as now
seemed almost certain, Arthur had had a mishap with
the dinghy, he could still have survived. His boat was
equipped with buoyancy bags and wouldn't have sunk
even if it had been overturned. The weather, though wet,
hadn't been at all rough, so he would probably have been
able to cling to the hull for some time and might easily
have been carried ashore somewhere, exhausted but alive.
Our best course was not to worry prematurely but to go
on looking. Carol nodded without speaking, and we set
off round the curving seaward shore of the island, gazing
tensely ahead as we opened up new stretches of the beach.
Actually I was prepared by now for anything—the second
oar, the dinghy—or a body. But there was nothing at all,
except the usual tidal fringe of seaweed and driftwood.

It was a hard two-mile plod to the end of the island.
From time to time we stopped and looked out to sea,
examining the smooth surface for a floating speck, but all
we could see were a few fishing boats in the misty distance.
After we'd combed the seaward side we walked back
along the inner side of the island, which was separated
from the mainland by a continuation of the Embery

Staithe creek. There were several smaller channels running deep into the dunes, where a dinghy might conceivably have been washed up, and we investigated them all, ploughing through deep mud. Finally we completed the circuit, and there was still nothing. The dinghy was definitely not there.

There was still no news when we got back to the house. I rang Sergeant Laycock and told him about the oar. He said it sounded bad, and promised they'd go on searching.

We spent a miserable afternoon. Fay's continued silence seemed inexplicable. Maureen was frightened, and near to tears. Carol looked ill with worry. After tea she suggested we should go out to the coast again for a last look round before dark, in case the dinghy had drifted in with the day's tide, but she looked so completely worn out after the nervous strain of the morning that I thought she'd better rest. To satisfy her, I said I'd go on my own, and left her with Maureen. I rowed out to the Point once more and climbed to the same look-out and again studied the coastline through my glasses. But all I could see were some men approaching along the edge of the bay—probably the search party.

I left them to it, and rowed across to the island and plunged into the sandhills, making for another high point from which I hoped to command a view of the curving beach without actually walking round it again. From the top I was in fact able to see almost to the end of the island—but again there was nothing. . . . Then, as I gazed around the undulating dunes that formed the interior, my eye was caught by the movement of something dark in the marram grass a hundred yards away. It looked like a bit of clothing. Puzzled, I set off to investigate.

As I drew nearer, I saw that it *was* clothing. It was a pair of blue bathing-trunks, spread out on the grass as though to dry. I quickened my step, plunging into little ravines and climbing again to sandy hillocks. And suddenly, in a hollow, I found Arthur!

He was lying on his face, fully-dressed but soaked and crumpled, with his hands flung out in front of him. He was quite motionless. Fighting my horror, I knelt and turned him over. He looked incredibly shrunken. The body was still slightly warm, but I could see that he was dead. There was no trace of a pulse, and his mouth and nose were filled with sand. So, I saw, were his fingernails, which were badly torn. Near the body were signs of vomiting.

I got unsteadily to my feet, gazing around. For a moment I couldn't imagine what had happened. I walked over to where the bathing-shorts were hanging. Close by them was another sheltered hollow which Arthur had evidently made his base. All his things were there—his picnic basket, with most of the food gone, his camera and binoculars, a rug, a book. The sand itself was in an incredible mess. The whole surface was churned up, as though Arthur had been desperately digging there. Near by I found other, similar, excavations. No wonder his nails had been broken! But *why* . . . ?

Suddenly I had a flash of intuition. I went back to the body and felt around in the soaking jacket pockets. Arthur's insulin and syringe weren't there. What I did find was a hole in the bottom of the left-hand pocket as big as my fist!

I knew, then, what must have happened. Arthur had lost his insulin somewhere in the sand. Panic-stricken, he'd burrowed for it, but hadn't been able to find it. He'd missed his vital evening dose and sunk gradually into a coma. Now, twenty-four hours later, he was dead.

So much was clear—but why hadn't he been able to leave the island before he needed the dose? What had happened to the dinghy? I could only suppose that he'd forgotten to put the anchor out, and that the rising tide had picked the boat up and carried it away, marooning him. For, of course, he couldn't swim.

It was too ghastly to think of. I could just imagine the hell he must have gone through—scrabbling wildly in one place after another for something that might have fallen anywhere, knowing he would probably die if he didn't find it, knowing the isolation of the place and the unlikelihood that he would be discovered in time. . . . Yet surely he could have lit a fire and made a signal . . . ? Then I remembered that he wasn't a smoker, that he probably didn't carry matches. There'd have been no way out for him. And by the time Carol and I had walked round the island at midday he'd have been too ill to show himself—probably he'd already have been in a coma. . . . If *only*, I thought, we'd searched the island then! But with no sign of the dinghy anywhere, there'd seemed no reason to. . . . Well, it was too late now for regrets.

I turned wretchedly away and started to walk back towards the boat. My mind was in a ferment. I wasn't thinking only of Arthur any more. I was thinking of Fay. She'd gone off somewhere, and hadn't bothered about him. She'd stayed away, all day and all night.

She'd virtually abandoned him. And there was that man who'd rung her, who'd called her " darling " . . . Was it possible she'd gone to *him*? It seemed incredible—and yet . . .

I was still thinking about it, in a confused way, when two of the men I'd seen on the beach beyond the Point appeared round the edge of the sandhills, deep in talk. I gave them a hail, and quickly rowed across to tell them what had happened. With their help, I'd be able to get Arthur home.

CHAPTER IX

IT TOOK us more than an hour to get the body off the island and row the heavily-laden boat back to the house. By then it was quite dark. One of the policemen went to the phone-box on the corner to summon the local doctor, a man named Franklin, and to make his report to the police station at Fairhaven. The other stayed with the boat while I went indoors to break the news. Carol was absolutely appalled when I told her. She'd been prepared for bad tidings about Arthur ever since we'd found the oar—but not for this. I gave her the facts as I knew them and we exchanged a few shocked, staccato words about it. Maureen was crying bitterly, and had to be calmed. Then the doctor arrived and gave Arthur's body a quick examination, making certain there was no spark of life left, and I answered a few questions. It turned out that Franklin was Fay's doctor, and of course he was concerned about her and asked where she was, and we had to tell him that we didn't know. We were still talking about it in the hall when the telephone rang in the sitting-room. I went to answer it.

It was Sergeant Laycock. He said, " Is that you, Mr. Renison? "

" Yes."

" Well, sir—I'm sorry, but I'm afraid we've got some more bad news for you. . . . It's Mrs. Ramsden. We've found her." His tone was grave.

" You don't mean . . . ? "

" Yes, sir—she's dead. She was drowned."

I sank into a chair. " Where . . . ? How . . . ? "

" She was caught up in the anchor of Mr. Ramsden's dinghy, sir. One of the fishing-smacks spotted the boat drifting off shore this afternoon, and it's just been brought in . . . Apparently it was carried out to sea with the anchor overboard, and she was dragged along with it . . . That's really all I can tell you at present . . . I'm extremely sorry about it, sir."

I said, " Well, thank you, Sergeant," and hung up. At that moment I'd only one thought in my mind— Carol. I knew it would shatter her. For a second I stood irresolutely. Then the door opened and Carol said, " What is it, James? " I saw with relief that Franklin was still with her.

I walked slowly towards her. I must have looked pretty awful, for she gave me one glance and the blood started to drain from her face. " Fay! " she said.

I nodded.

She swayed, and I leapt forward and caught her and laid her gently on the ground. She had passed right out. I said to Franklin, " Her sister's been drowned." He said, " Oh, dear, oh, dear! " ministering to her on the floor with something from his black bag. Presently we carried her upstairs and put her on the bed. She came round after a little while, but it was almost worse than if she hadn't. She was in a frightful state, shuddering and sobbing and almost beside herself. In the end Franklin had to give her an injection to quieten her, and then she went off to sleep.

" She should be all right," he said. " It's been a very bad shock, but she's strong and healthy—if she has complete rest and quiet she ought to be over the worst in a few days. . . . What happened, Mr. Renison? " He looked pretty shocked himself.

I told him the little I knew about the accident, and we talked for a few minutes. He was a silver-haired, elderly man, with kind but shrewd eyes and an air of quiet authority. I felt he was a man I could have full confidence in. He said he'd call again first thing in the morning, and I thanked him.

Soon after he'd gone, a police ambulance arrived and took Arthur's body away to the mortuary at Fairhaven. I was a little surprised, though in all the circumstances it seemed the best thing. The two policemen said good night and left. I gave Maureen some aspirin and did my best to console her—she'd obviously been very fond both of Arthur and Fay—and sent her off to bed. Then I sat on downstairs, thinking about things—about Fay, and the man who'd rung her up, and what she'd been doing in the dinghy at all. But I was too exhausted to try and get any more information that night.

Franklin was round next morning before Carol was properly out of her drugged sleep. He checked her over and said that she was doing all right but that he was going to keep her under sedatives for a bit. I went and sat with her for a while after breakfast, holding her hand, which was all the comfort I could give her—while the tears rolled slowly down her cheeks. I felt deeply anxious about her—and in spite of what Franklin had said I guessed he was more concerned than he'd seemed. There'd been cases, I knew, where one identical twin had been unable to face life alone after the death of the other —where melancholia and even suicide had followed. From what I'd seen of Carol she was too strong-minded a person to give way so utterly to despair, but this twin business was trickier than most relationships and I felt responsibility heavy upon me. I was, for the moment, almost literally all she had in the world.

She was still dopy, and very soon she went off to sleep again and I left her. At ten I rang John Allenby at the F.O. and told him briefly of the double tragedy and the fix I was in. He was very sympathetic and said I wasn't to worry about coming in until I'd got everything straightened out. I could only guess what his private thoughts were—what with holidays, honeymoons and tragedies I was turning out a pretty poor investment for the Foreign Office. But I'd too much on my mind to worry about that now. I telephoned Mother and told her what had happened, so that she wouldn't hear about it first from the newspapers, and of course she was appalled, and terribly sorry for Carol, and she offered to come up to Norfolk right away and lend a hand. Something must have warned me against that—anyway, I said it wasn't really necessary, that everything was under control, and that I'd keep in touch. . . . I was about to ring Sergeant Laycock after that to see if I could get more details of the accident, but he rang me instead and asked me if I could go in for a talk at three that afternoon, and

I said I would. Maureen, who was bearing up pretty well by now, got some lunch for us, and in the afternoon I left her in charge of Carol and drove into Fairhaven.

I was shown straight into a private office at the police station. Sergeant Laycock was there, with another man in plain clothes whom he introduced as Detective-Inspector Burns, of the county C.I.D. I couldn't imagine what his interest was in the affair. He shook hands with me, and offered me a chair, and after a moment Laycock left us alone.

" Well, this is a bad business, Mr. Renison," Burns said. " A *very* bad business. . . ." He was a heavily-built man of middle age, with a quiet, almost apologetic manner, and a penetrating eye. " How is your wife this morning? "

" A little better," I said, " thank you."

" I understand that she and Mrs. Ramsden were twins."

" Yes—identical twins, and very close. Fay's death has been a fearful blow to her."

" I can well imagine . . ." Burns sighed. " Well, now, if you'll allow me there are just one or two questions I'd like to ask you. . . . I gather that you and your wife came up to Norfolk on Saturday afternoon? "

" Yes—we got here about five-thirty."

" Did the Ramsdens know you were coming? "

" No—my wife had a kind of presentiment that something might be wrong, and as we couldn't get through on the telephone we came up to see. . . . It was a sudden decision."

" I see . . ." For some reason, Burns seemed to find that a satisfactory answer. " And what was the position when you got here? "

I told him how we'd found the house empty, the Daimler in the garage, and the dinghy missing; I told him of Maureen's return, and what she'd said about Arthur having gone out alone early and Fay's shopping plans, and of our increasing disquiet as the weather got worse. Burns listened carefully.

" Yes," he said at the end. " Well, that all fits—and now I can fill in the picture for you. Mrs. Ramsden did go shopping—she was seen in the town here with the car. Afterwards she returned to the house, garaged the car, and walked out to the Point. She changed there into a swim-suit she'd taken with her, and swam across to the island. Mr. Ramsden's dinghy would have been on the island side, of course. . . . She was still wearing the swim-suit when she was picked up by the fishing-boat—and this morning we found her clothes in a hollow at the Point. So her movements are quite clear."

I nodded. So far, it made sense. Fay had evidently changed her mind about going to the island, and had followed Arthur out. " But how on earth did she get caught up in the dinghy anchor? " I asked. " What do you suppose she was doing? "

" If you'll allow me," Burns said, " I'll come to that in a moment." His tone had become even more apologetic—he was the politest policeman I'd ever met. " You know, of course, what the cause of Mr. Ramsden's death was, don't you? "

" Yes—not having his insulin. He lost it through a hole in his pocket. . . ."

Burns slowly shook his head. " We had a good look at that hole, Mr. Renison. The material of the pocket was in pretty good condition—not in the least rotten. It had been ripped. Deliberately . . . Mr. Ramsden didn't *lose* his insulin. It was taken from him."

I stared at him incredulously.

" We found it," Burns said, " in the dinghy—in Mrs. Ramsden's handbag." He reached down behind him and produced a cardboard box with a collection of articles in it. One of them was a green handbag which I recognised as Fay's. From the bag, Burns extracted a small pouch, like a tobacco pouch, and displayed the contents—a hypodermic syringe, a small bottle of soluble insulin, and some cotton-wool. " There you are," he said. " All Mr. Ramsden's vital equipment."

For a moment I was speechless. Then I said, " Inspector, are you suggesting that my sister-in-law took her husband's insulin away from him, and tore his pocket to make the loss seem accidental, and deliberately left him on the island to die . . . ? "

" I'm afraid so," Burns said quietly.

" But it's monstrous . . . ! It's the most infamous suggestion I ever heard. . . ."

He sighed again. " If she didn't, how did the insulin come to be in her bag? "

" She was taking it to him, of course. He must have forgotten it. . . ."

" *Did* he ever forget it? "

" He must have done this time. . . . She came back to the house, and found it there, and took it out to him."

" If it was as simple as that," Burns said, " wouldn't she in fact have joined him? Would she have stopped and messed about with the dinghy? And why should the pocket have been ripped? "

" There must be some other explanation of that. . . ."

Burns shook his head again. " The only explanation that covers all the facts is the one I've given you. . . . I realise, Mr. Renison, how painful all this must be to you, but somebody in the family had to be told. . . . It's really quite clear what happened. Arthur Ramsden went for a bathe that morning—we know that from the fact that his swimming-trunks were hung up to dry. It seems likely that Mrs. Ramsden reached his base in the sandhills while he was down by the sea. She took the insulin from his coat, tore the pocket, and returned to the dinghy, intending to set it adrift and so give the impression that her husband hadn't secured it properly. She got the anchor up and started to row the boat across the channel. In her nervous excitement she lost an oar —the one you found. She tried to anchor the boat again while she recovered it. Something went wrong—perhaps she slipped. Anyway, she fell overboard, and the anchor caught in the strap of her swim-suit as she fell. She wasn't able to disentangle it, and she was drowned, and the dinghy drifted out to sea with her. That's how she was found—in tow, so to speak. . . . Anyhow, that's our reconstruction."

I sat in a cold sweat, looking at him. " It *can't* be true," I said. " She'd never have done it—it's fantastic. Utterly fantastic. She was devoted to Arthur. . . ." I broke off.

Burns was regarding me thoughtfully. " Would you say there were no domestic difficulties? I'd like the truth, Mr. Renison."

I hesitated, but only for a moment. He'd probably heard rumours—and in any case he'd be able to get all the information he wanted from Maureen. I said, " There were difficulties, yes—but they were caused entirely by Arthur."

" What did you understand was the trouble? "

" He'd taken to going out alone at night, and Fay had followed him once or twice. On one occasion she thought he was meeting someone, and I believe they had words about it afterwards. She was worried about him—that's all."

" I take it this is what Mrs. Ramsden told you? "

" She told my wife, yes."

" Did either of you ever discuss it with Arthur Ramsden himself? "

" Well, no—it would have been difficult. . . ." I suddenly remembered that Carol had wanted to do just that, and that Fay had asked her not to.

" That's what I thought," Burns said. " I'm afraid, Mr. Renison, you accepted Mrs. Ramsden's one-sided account too readily. It seems much more likely that it was *she* who was meeting someone—and Arthur Ramsden who was following *her*. She had a man friend, you know."

" I can't believe that. . . ."

" You say you can't, but I think you must do. . . . I understand there was a telephone call for Mrs. Ramsden the night you arrived. Sergeant Laycock tells me a man rang up, a man none of you knew. He said something like, ' Did you manage it, darling? ' and then hurriedly rang off when he found it wasn't Mrs. Ramsden he was speaking to. That doesn't sound to me like devotion on Mrs. Ramsden's part. It sounds exactly as though she was having an affair with a man and—in view of every-thing else—that they had plotted together to kill her husband. He wanted to know if she'd managed it—and she had! "

I groaned. " It's not possible . . . I'm sure you're imagining things. . . . That call could have meant anything."

" It's not the only evidence we have," Burns said

quietly. "We found a note in her handbag. . . ." He opened the bag again and took out a small piece of paper that looked as though it had been torn from a loose-leaf note-book. On it, written in pencil in a neat Italian script, were the words, "I hate leaving it all to you, darling. Good luck! I'll ring you to-night."

I read it through twice, rigid with horror. I couldn't think of a word to say.

"Well, Mr. Renison?"

I still couldn't believe it. "It just doesn't make sense," I said. "Good God, Inspector, even if Fay *did* have a lover she could have gone off with him without plotting to kill her husband. . . ."

"Your loyalty does you credit," Burns said grimly, "but aren't you being a little naïve? Mr. Ramsden was a very rich man. I've been talking to his solicitor—it seems likely that the estate will total well over two hundred thousand pounds, and apart from a few minor bequests it's all willed to Mrs. Ramsden. If she'd left her husband for someone else, obviously he'd have changed his will. As it was, she and the boy friend would have been able to enjoy the inheritance together if it hadn't been for the mishap—the rather fortunate mishap, I would say—that killed her, too."

I was silent.

"So you see," Burns went on, "it all fits. I can well understand your reluctance to believe it, but there's absolutely no question about it. Even the smallest things tie in. For instance, there's Mrs. Ramsden's story about having important things to do in Fairhaven that morning. Obviously it was just an excuse, so that she could let her husband get ahead of her to the island and follow him later, secretly."

E

" You can't *know* it was an excuse," I said.

" Oh, but we do. We've checked very thoroughly on
her movements that morning. She parked her car on
the quay at about ten o'clock. She was watched by three
old pensioners who always sit on the seat there—you may
have noticed them. Ten minutes later she returned to
the car and drove away. In those ten minutes she bought
half a pound of ham and some tea and collected some
snapshots from the chemist. And that's all. Perhaps
you'd like to look at the snaps. . . ." Burns tossed a
yellow packet across to me. " They were in her bag.
Would *you* say they were important? "

I glanced through them. They were the usual things
—Arthur in the dinghy, several of Fay sun-bathing on the
beach, a couple of indoor shots of the house, a few birds.
Nothing of the least significance.

I passed them back. " There may have been something else. . . . Perhaps her important business wasn't
actually in Fairhaven."

" She *said* Fairhaven—and if there was anything else it
must have been transacted remarkably quickly. The
boatmen at Embery Staithe says the car was back at the
house by ten-thirty."

He had an answer to everything.

I glanced into the cardboard box to see if there were
any other exhibits. There was what looked like one of
Arthur's used flashlight bulbs. I said, " Has that got
anything to do with anything? "

" No—it just happened to be in the bilges when we
cleared out the dinghy." Burns got to his feet. " Well,
Mr. Renison, that's the case. . . . It's not been pleasant
having to tell you, but I thought you'd better know."

I got up in a kind of daze. I *still* couldn't believe it.

I said, " I just can't *see* Fay Ramsden doing a thing like that. . . ."

Burns said, " How long have you known her, Mr. Renison? "

" About five months."

He gave a little nod. " It's not very long, is it? "

CHAPTER X

I DROVE back to the house in a state of indescribable mental anguish. I felt torn apart, as instinctive disbelief warred with the bleak, unanswerable facts. Until Burns had produced his array of proof, I'd have staked my life on Fay's innocence. I'd as soon have believed that the sun could fall out of the sky. Yet the evidence was overwhelming, and I couldn't disregard it.

All the same, I didn't accept it without a lot more questioning. The moment I got in I asked Maureen if she could remember anything having been said about Arthur's insulin on the Saturday morning. If she couldn't, it would be something—a straw to clutch at. But she remembered only too well. The usual routine had been followed. As Arthur had left the house she had heard Fay call out, " Got your stuff, darling? " and seen Arthur give his pocket the customary tap. So that was that. I asked her if she had heard either Arthur or Fay say anything about a pocket that needed repairing, and she said she hadn't. Another broken straw.

I asked her to tell me all she could about the night walks that Arthur and Fay had taken, but her answers gave me no comfort. There had been, she thought, three or four

occasions at intervals of a few weeks when someone had
gone out late. The last time had been on the Thursday
night, two days before the fatality, when she thought
both of them had been out. That, Burns would probably
say, had been the time when Fay and her lover had met
to put the final touches to their plan. I asked Maureen
if she could remember who had gone out first on these
nocturnal trips, since that was crucial—but she couldn't.
She'd always been in bed, apparently, and had had only
a vague, sleepy impression of goings and comings. I
asked her if she'd ever heard Fay and Arthur quarrelling,
and if so whether she knew what the quarrels had been
about. She said she *had* heard slightly raised voices once
or twice, but she'd no idea who'd been blaming whom,
or for what.

So Burns's case remained completely intact. There
was no evidence at all, except the dead Fay's, that it was
Arthur's actions which had started the domestic trouble
—and plenty that it was Fay's. Arthur had obviously
become suspicious of Fay and tried to find out what she
was up to, as any jealous husband might do. . . .

Suspicious of Fay . . . ? For one moment, casting my
mind back, I thought I had found a weakness in the case
after all. I remembered again how warmly Arthur had
talked of Fay at our first meeting—how he had gone out
of his way to praise her as the perfect wife. He would
never have done that if he'd had the slightest doubt about
her fidelity. . . . Then I realised that our talk had probably preceded the first of the night walks. At that time,
Arthur would have had, at most, a vague sense of lessened
affection. That would have accounted for his hungry
look, his moments of preoccupation. The feeling, barely
realised, might well have led him, too, to stress Fay's

devotion in his talk with me—a sort of verbal reassurance for himself, a whistling to keep his courage up. Poor devil! I could still see the deep emotion on his face as he'd said, " She means everything to me." In retrospect, it was pitiful.

Then, for a brief moment, disbelief returned. I remembered that it was Fay who had first mentioned the domestic trouble, who had told Carol of the night walks. Would she have done that, if she herself had started everything by going out to meet a lover? Wouldn't she have kept quiet about the whole thing . . . ? But when I thought about it a little more, I could see just how clever she'd been. She'd have known, by then, that Arthur was suspicious—she'd have known that at some point *he* might talk to us. So she'd got her own account in first, throwing doubts even on his mental stability with her story of his praying in the sand, conditioning us so that in a show-down we'd believe her and not him and be unsuspicious when he died. . . . Yes, she'd been clever.

I continued to wrestle with the facts—but it was a losing battle. The old picture of Fay, loving and solicitous, was steadily fading—the new one was taking convincing shape. The plain truth was that I'd been completely fooled by her—and now I could see it. Indeed, the disillusionment had started, I supposed, with that secret phone call to her, which I'd tried to make light of at the time but had worried about all the same. It had been pretty clear then that she hadn't been all she'd appeared to be. Now other things came crowding into my mind. I remembered how I hadn't been able to understand what she'd been able to see in Arthur to make her want to marry him—how I'd had to fall back on the old maternal instinct to explain it. But of course she'd simply married him for his money. I remembered the early see-saw of poverty and luxury that could so easily have given her a loathing of the one, a determination to seek the other at all costs. I remembered the picture that Arthur had drawn of her parents—the drunken father, the worthless mother. The mother who'd *also* married money! How wrong he'd been about Fay inheriting only their best characteristics!

It was true what Burns had said—I hadn't known Fay long enough—or well enough. I'd taken the façade of kindness and devotion for the whole, forgetting that she was an actress and that outward appearances were nothing to go by. I knew better now. Obviously she had merely pretended solicitude for her rich, middle-aged, ailing husband, while planning all the time to get rid of him and enjoy his money with someone else.

Horror returned once more, as I thought of what she'd done. She must have been a woman utterly without feeling, utterly inhuman—vile. If all had gone according to plan, she would have been talking happily to her lover on the telephone at the very moment when Arthur was breaking his nails on the sand in anguish and despair. The monstrous callousness was almost beyond belief. But that, I could no longer doubt, was what Fay had been—a calculating little monster, with a lovely face and black poison in her veins. The plot, from first to last, had been diabolically evil. It would give me nightmares for years to come.

Yet it wasn't Fay and her wickedness that mono-polised my thoughts any more. In the forefront of my mind there was now a racking anxiety about Carol. For I couldn't forget that she and Fay had come from the same stock and the same background; that according to

Carol they'd been identical in every way; that Carol had also been an actress; that she, too, had married a wealthy man; and that I hadn't known her for very long, either!

CHAPTER XI

THE NEXT few days were an unrelieved ordeal. The sinister facts had quickly leaked out and everyone in the district was talking in hushed horror about Fay and—as I imagined—about Carol, too. The double tragedy, with its unique and sensational features, had naturally become headline news in the Press, and reporters from all over the country had flocked to Embery Staithe, turning the sea wall and island into a busy promenade and the creek into a dinghy park. As Fay was dead, they could discuss the case with almost no inhibitions, and they did. In all the circumstances, I could hardly blame them. They weren't able to reach Carol, but their papers found plenty of material about the sisters without that—stuff from old variety magazines and, of course, photographs. Whatever newspaper I looked at, there were photographs—hauntingly, terrifyingly alike. I excited quite a lot of attention myself, too, as the husband of the surviving twin, and men with cameras repeatedly snapped me as I moved around. Most of the reporters were staying at the hotel opposite the house, so I was under almost constant siege and observation. I'd gladly have escaped with Carol to London, but Franklin thought she shouldn't be put to the strain of a journey for a day or two, and Burns wanted me to stay, and in any case I knew

I'd have to be around for the inquest. So we stayed. Franklin had put an absolute ban on Carol being told the truth about the tragedy yet, on the principle that it was better to get over one shock before being subjected to another and greater one. She asked very few questions, which was a measure of her prostration. For hours at a time she just lay, white, motionless and staring into space, showing no interest in anything. On one point, at least, I could have no doubts—her grief was genuine. As to the other question, I tried as far as was humanly possible to put it out of my mind until she was re-covered.

On the first evening, after my talk with Maureen, I'd composed a letter to my parents, to reach them before the news broke. It was one of the hardest letters I'd ever written in my life. I knew how devastated they'd be—and I knew so well what Mother would think. She'd never really attempted to hide her view that I'd married un-wisely and with precipitate haste into a highly dubious family. Within months, her worst forebodings had been more than realised. Yet out of love and loyalty to Carol —or perhaps from sheer pride—I wasn't prepared to concede a thing beyond the facts. In the end I just told her what had happened and left it at that. I asked her not to come to Norfolk, or even to telephone me for a day or two, as I didn't feel able to discuss anything. I knew her too well to imagine there'd be even a hint of " I told you so " in her manner, but I didn't want sympathy, either, or anything else—I just wanted to work out my own salvation, if I ever could, in my own way. . . . Twenty-four hours later I got a letter back from her. It must have been even more difficult to write than mine. Inevitably it showed shock and pain, and deep anxiety about me, and regret over not being able to do anything, but on the whole it was amazingly restrained. It ended on the note that they both understood how I felt and that if I should need help or comfort at any time they were always there. It was a wonderful letter, and it moved me deeply.

I dispatched one other letter that first evening—to John Allenby. I'd always enjoyed my work at the Foreign Office, and I had a feeling it might mean even more to me in the future, but I'd no doubt about the course I had to take. I knew that during the next few days the glare of publicity would be full on me, and that the fact that I was a Foreign Office man wouldn't go unmentioned. I knew how embarrassing the F.O. always found that sort of thing. I told Allenby briefly what had happened and that it was bound to be splashed in the papers, and asked him to consider that he had my resignation on his desk if he wanted it. He wrote back expressing his deep regret at my news, thanking me for my letter, and saying that he saw no need at the moment for any drastic step and that I could have leave of absence until the position became clearer. The decencies had been preserved on both sides.

I was so fully occupied during the next two days that I had little chance to dwell on my personal problem, even if I'd wanted to. Apart from keeping a watchful eye on Carol, I had to see Arthur's Norwich solicitor, a quiet, friendly little man named Hamilton, and also make some private arrangements about the coming inquest. I had several talks with Burns, too. The police, naturally, were very interested in Fay's lover—far more so than in Fay, for she was dead and beyond the reach of the law, while he was still alive and at large. The inspector had

hoped at one time that he might learn something from
the footprints on the island, but what with the trampling
that had gone on during the search for Arthur and the
recovery of the body, and the heavy rain that had fallen
all through the night of the murder, the picture had become hopelessly confused. The note in Fay's bag might
serve as a possible handwriting check if a suspect could
ever be found, though the writing on the note gave the
impression of having been heavily disguised and with such
a small sample to work on a conclusive identification
would be most unlikely. There was, of course, the man's
voice on the telephone, and Burns asked me to describe
it. I told him what I could—that it had been deep, and
rather breathless, and that the accent had been cultured
—but he'd already had that from Sergeant Laycock and
there was nothing I could add. You can't really describe
a voice, and anyway my recollection was very vague.
The police were also doing a good deal of questioning in
the village, hoping they might find someone who had
actually seen Fay with a strange man at some time—but
they had no success. It was hardly surprising, for the
assignations would always have been after dark—though
I did wonder how and where she'd met him in the first
place. A possibility, I thought, was that he'd been a
casual visitor in the early summer and that Fay had met
him by chance on the sea wall or out at the Point and got
into conversation with him and allowed things to develop
from there. He was certainly a mysterious figure—so
mysterious that I'd still have found it hard to believe in
his existence if I hadn't myself heard his voice and seen
the note he'd written. On the whole, it seemed to me
most unlikely that he'd ever be brought to book. If the
plot had gone according to plan, he'd presumably have

stayed in the background until everything had blown
over and then joined Fay somewhere to share the spoils.
As it was, he'd obviously stay in the background for
ever.

CHAPTER XII

THE DOUBLE inquest was held in Fairhaven in a hall
packed to the doors with Press and public. The pro-
ceedings were expected to last all day, and as Maureen
and I would both have to give evidence, Franklin had
arranged for a nurse to go in and look after Carol. In
addition to Hamilton, who was keeping an eye on things
as Arthur's executor, I'd got a solicitor down from
London to represent the relatives—Carol and myself.
He was a man named Ffoulkes, from a well-known firm
of criminal lawyers, and he impressed me favourably—
though in fact I knew that his presence could hardly be
more than a formality. After we had gone over all the
evidence together, his view had been that there would be
little for him to do.

I'd never attended an inquest before, and many things
about it surprised me—particularly its slowness, the long
pauses while the evidence was written down, and the fact
that the coroner seemed to make up his own rules of
procedure as he went along. But out of what sometimes
appeared to be a very untidy inquiry, a picture emerged
in the end which was only too clear.

First, there were the medical reports. The one on
Arthur showed that he'd died as a result of circulatory
collapse following severe ketosis due to lack of insulin—

which, the doctor said, he might well have needed in even larger quantities than usual as he'd spent a comparatively restful day on the island and burned up little body-sugar. Worry over his wife could also have increased his insulin need. There had been recorded cases, the doctor said, of full coma developing within eight hours of missing one large dose of soluble insulin, and many within twenty-four hours. The time of death in Arthur's case was clearly established as the late afternoon of the second day. The report on Fay confirmed that she had been drowned. A few minor bruises on her were consistent with her struggle to free herself from the dinghy anchor before death. There was some doubt about exactly when she had died, but it had certainly been on the first day and not the second and she'd therefore predeceased Arthur, which was all the lawyers were interested in. I gave evidence of finding Arthur's body and described the scene. A fisherman gave similar evidence about finding Fay and the dinghy.

Then, by means of police statements and a mosaic of evidence from the various people involved, the pattern of events was slowly built up. There was the deteriorated relationship between Fay and Arthur, the beginning of the night walks, the never-very-convincing explanation that Fay had given of them, the much more likely hypo-thesis that she'd initiated them herself, and—a new point —the reluctance she'd shown about going to stay with her sister in London, which Arthur had no doubt suggested to test her, to see if she could tear herself away from Norfolk, which she couldn't. Then came the fact that, though usually she had accompanied her husband on his outings, on the fatal day she had chosen to stay behind and go into Fairhaven without any substantial reason;

and that immediately afterwards she had walked to the
Point and swum to the island, as was proved by the finding
of her clothes. After that there was an expert's view of
the phony tear in Arthur's jacket pocket, which the jury
were invited to examine for themselves; a verbal reconstruction by Burns of the dinghy accident, which could
so easily have been caused by over-eagerness on Fay's
part to set the boat adrift and get away; an account of
the discovery of the insulin in Fay's bag and Maureen's
evidence that Arthur had taken it with him that morning;
the production of the damning written message, and
evidence of the even more damning phone call. Finally,
reference to Arthur's will supplied the motive for the
whole ghoulish business. It was more than just an inquest
—it was a posthumous prosecution.

Ffoulkes, doing his best in a hopeless cause, asked a
number of pertinent questions of the police, but Burns
had all the answers. Ffoulkes wanted to know just how
and when it was supposed that Fay had received the
message which had been found in her bag. The note, he
said, had mentioned telephoning " to-night," which
indicated that it had been written on the fatal day and
therefore couldn't have been delivered by post. How had
she got it? But the inspector had already worked that
one out. His idea was that Fay's lover had himself been
in the vicinity of the Point earlier that day; that, not
wishing to risk being seen with Fay, he had left the note
for her in some hiding place they were accustomed to use,
by way of last-minute encouragement; and that she had
picked it up on her way out. Ffoulkes asked why, if the
lover had been around, he had left it to Fay to do the
dirty work. Burns reasonably replied that Fay would
have had a much better chance of quietly abstracting the

insulin than a stranger. While it was well on the cards
that the insulin had in fact been taken while Arthur was
down at the sea, bathing, that was only a hypothesis, and
certainly no one could have counted on such a thing.
A wife would have had little difficulty in rifling her
husband's pocket at any time—for instance, while he had
lain dozing beside her in the sandhills with his jacket
thrown aside. A stranger would have had no such opportunity. The coroner gave an approving nod at that, and
returned to his notes.

Ffoulkes came nearest to making an impression when
he asked what it was supposed that Fay's plan would
have been if all had gone well and she had not had her
accident with the dinghy. Clearly, he said, once Arthur's
body had been found, an exhaustive search would have
been made for the insulin, the loss of which had caused his
death. Failure to find it might have aroused suspicion.
Had Fay planned to take it back to the island later and
drop it in the sand—and if so, when? She couldn't have
hoped to do it during daylight, while her husband was
still alert and well. And once she had given the alarm,
which for appearances' sake she would certainly have had
to do that evening when Arthur didn't come home, she
would have been involved with police and search parties
and would have had no further opportunity for secretly
replacing the insulin. . . . Apart from that, there'd have
been the obvious risk for the conspirators that a search
party going out early in the morning would have found
Arthur still alive—as in fact he had been—and restorable,
in which case the plot would not only have failed in its
purpose but would probably have been detected, since
Arthur would have known not only that he had left his
dinghy quite secure but that there had been no hole in his

pocket. And incidentally, Ffoulkes added, wouldn't the conspirators have been afraid that the deliberate nature of the tear might have been discovered in any evént? In short, had this plot really been a promising one?—and if it hadn't, would it have been undertaken?

At that point the coroner, looking startled, asked Ffoulkes if he was seeking to throw doubt on the genuineness of the evidence that had been heard. Ffoulkes replied blandly that he wasn't doing that—he was merely trying to clear up certain obscurities. The ball then passed to the inspector.

Burns, in his quiet way, was more than equal to the occasion. He lacked the lawyer's court technique, but he'd been longer with the case and knew it backwards. Any theory about how the conspirators had viewed later developments, he said—I'm paraphrasing him—must be purely speculative, since the man was not available for questioning, and Fay was dead; but he'd given a good deal of thought to the matter and he'd come to the conclusion that the difficulties and dangers mentioned wouldn't have been serious enough to have deterred such skilful and daring plotters. As far as the risk of Arthur being discovered alive was concerned, there would have seemed little chance of that. The plotters would have known that once the searchers had failed to find Arthur's dinghy at the island they would assume that Arthur wasn't there either and would concentrate on the sea and the beaches, which was precisely what had happened. And Arthur, even if not dead, would have been in no condition by that time to attract attention to himself. . . . As to the question of how the insulin could have been safely restored to the island, if that had been the intention, there were at least two ways in which the conspirators might have decided it could be done. One was that Fay could have arranged to be with the search party when it finally got around to combing the island—and nothing would have been easier than for her to detach herself for a moment and drop the insulin in the sand for someone else to find. Or, alternatively, she could have cached it the first evening in a prearranged place on the mainland—perhaps in the place where the note had been left—and her lover could have collected it and swum out to the island under cover of darkness and dropped it in the sand himself. Once it had been found on the island, everyone would have accepted without question that Arthur's death had been the result of its accidental loss, and no one would have thought of doubting the genuineness of the hole in the pocket. . . . In short, if Fay hadn't had her mishap with the boat the conspirators' plan would in all probability have met with complete success. . . .

It was a convincing reply, and there was little more to be said. Ffoulkes had clearly shot his bolt, and was sitting back with the air of a man who'd done his best with quite inadequate material. It remained only for the coroner to sum up. He was rather wordy, but he left no doubt in anyone's mind about what he thought. He concluded by reminding the jury of their responsibility. It had been a shocking, a terrible affair, he said, and members of the jury, many of whom had known the Ramsdens, might well feel that it was a most distasteful duty they had to fulfil. But fulfil it they must.

They did. The verdict on Fay was " Misadventure "; on Arthur, that he had been wilfully murdered by his wife and an unknown man.

CHAPTER XIII

THE FUNERAL followed two days later. After consulting Hamilton, and with the permission of the authorities, I'd taken upon myself the responsibility of arranging that both Arthur and Fay should be cremated and their ashes scattered. It seemed the best way of ending the whole dreadful business. Quite a number of local people attended the service for Arthur. Only Franklin, Hamilton and I stood by as Fay's remains were lowered to the flames. Franklin, with my approval, had decided to keep Carol under sedatives until the funeral was over, so there was no question of her going. Because of the dope, she was still apathetic and submissive. She'd asked me the night before, in a drowsy tone, what had happened at the inquest, and I'd told her the half-truth that the verdict had been " Misadventure," without going into details. I'd also mentioned that Fay was to be cremated, and she'd nodded, and not questioned me further.

On the day after the funeral I cleared up at the house and settled the last of our affairs in the district. Maureen, with a final burst of tears, departed for the nearby village where her family lived. She'd been a real brick, and I felt immeasurably grateful for all she'd done. We said good-bye to Franklin, and left the key of the house at the village shop as Hamilton had asked us to do, and by noon we were on our way back to London. Carol was quiet, but now it was the quietness of sad reflection, not of drugs. For the first time since Fay's death she was physically almost back to normal, and mentally composed without outside aids, and I knew the moment was at hand when I'd have to tell her the whole truth. I dreaded it, and yet I longed for it. The impact might well be fearful—yet I could scarcely wait to hear what she had to say about herself and Fay. Whatever my reason might tell me, I was still deeply under her spell and ready to seize on any reassurance she could give me. She, if anyone could, should be able to find some factor, until now overlooked, which had distorted the character of one twin and passed the other by.

It was Carol herself who gave me the opening I needed. As we sat over coffee that evening, the inhibiting curtain of melancholy which had wrapped her round all day seemed to part for a moment, giving way to a healthier curiosity. "James," she said, "tell me more about the inquest. What happened?"

So there it was! I took a deep breath, and said, "A great many things happened . . . I've been wanting to tell you, but Dr. Franklin thought I'd better wait a few days. Now you've got to know."

"Know what?"

"Fay wasn't what you thought her, Carol. She wasn't what any of us thought. She was bad—worse than you can imagine. . . . Carol, I wish to heaven I didn't have to say this—you must try and keep a grip on yourself. . . . The truth is, Fay was responsible for Arthur's death."

Carol looked at me uncomprehendingly.

"She and that man who rang her up—they had a plan —a plot. . . . He was her boy friend. They'd planned to get rid of Arthur so that they could have his money as well as each other. Arthur died because Fay took his

insulin away and left him on the island without
it."

There was a short, dreadful silence. Carol was staring
at me as though she thought I'd gone quite mad.

" I know it must sound utterly fantastic to you," I said.
"When I first heard it I couldn't believe it, either. I
fought against it. . . . But it's true. It's all in the papers.
Everything came out at the inquest. The verdict was
' Murder '."

I watched her, waiting. I was prepared for anything.
Total collapse wouldn't have surprised me. Neither would
some extravagant act. But she merely looked dazed. She
seemed not to have taken it in properly. I got up and
fetched one of the papers from the bundle that had
accumulated at the flat in our absence, and spread it out
in front of her. It had twin pictures of her and Fay on
the front page, and the story under big headlines. She
started to read, a look of utter incredulity on her face.
As she got the gist of it, incredulity changed to outrage.
Suddenly she exploded.

" How *dare* they . . . ! Of all the wicked lies . . . ! "

" I know how you must feel . . ." I began gently—
though in fact I didn't.

She cut me short, her face hard with anger. I'd never
seen her remotely like that before. " You're not telling
me *you* believe this? "

" Carol, I have to believe it. . . . It's the truth."

" Of course it's not the truth. It's absolute nonsense,
the whole lot of it. . . . Fay would never have done a
thing like that."

" But she did, Carol. It's been proved. You've only
skimmed the surface—the evidence is all there. You can't
get away from it."

" It's rubbish, I tell you."

" You only think that because it's Fay. If it were anyone else. . . ."

She got up and went away from me, away to the other side of the room, and stood there, looking at me in the strangest way. " I don't understand you," she said slowly. " You knew Fay. You liked her. How *can* you believe such monstrous things. . . . And if you can believe them of her, what must you think of me? "

" What Fay did is nothing to do with you," I said. Even as I framed the words, it struck me as one of the world's stupidest remarks.

" It's everything to do with me. Aren't you forgetting we were exactly alike? "

" You were alike in many ways," I said, struggling on, " but obviously not in all. . . ."

She shook her head. " You're wrong—we were alike in everything that counted. I told you so before. We were two of a kind. We *thought* alike. If it had been possible for us to exchange brains, I doubt if we'd even have known the exchange had been made. *That's* how alike we were."

I groaned inwardly. Everything was going wrong. Far from giving me the reassurance I'd wanted, she was stoking my anxieties.

" Something must have been different," I repeated. " Something you don't know about, perhaps. A prenatal influence—some sort of physical pressure before birth. . . ." I was groping wildly in an unknown land. " Or some damage to her *at* birth. . . . Carol, there must have been something." I was pleading with her now.

" There wasn't anything," she said stonily. " We were both perfectly normal, healthy babies, exactly alike."

" Then there was some external thing—something that changed her. . . ."

" I tell you there was nothing. We were brought up together, we shared the same influences, we had the same experiences—we even had the same illnesses. Nothing important ever happened to her that didn't happen to me."

" She met this man," I said, because it was the only thing I could think of.

" Would that have changed her from being a decent, ordinary girl into the she-devil these papers describe?"

" It must have done. She came under his influence. . . ."

" Nonsense! I'd have known."

" She was a good actress, Carol. She managed to deceive you. . . ."

" God! You simply don't know what you're talking about. . . . We *couldn't* have deceived each other, about anything."

" It happened," I said. " It's no good saying it couldn't have done, because it did. . . . It's all here in the paper, in black and white."

" Black and white! It's just lies! " She gave me a bitter look. " All I can say is, if you believe that of her you're certainly taking a big chance with me. If you were so wrong about her, what makes you think I'm genuine? How do you know *I'm* not waiting for a chance to get rid of *you* and share your money with someone I like better? Why should you trust me. . .? I can't believe the thought hasn't occurred to you."

" Of course it's occurred to me," I said. " It would to anyone who wasn't a complete fool. . . . What I want is to have it disproved."

" Then you're asking the impossible. You'd better go

away and read up about identical twins—there's a lot more in the subject than I've ever told you. Read about *criminal* twins—there've been some fascinating case histories. . . . There was a man who studied thirteen pairs of identical twins where one of the twins was a known criminal. Do you know what he found? In ten cases the second twin was a criminal, too!"

"There were still the other three cases," I said desperately.

"Fay and I wouldn't have been among them. We'd have been among the ten. Fay and I were replicas. . . . So whatever you think about her, you must think about me, too."

"I won't—I can't. . . ."

"You must. If you believe she was capable of murder, then you must believe I am. If you don't believe I am, then you can't believe she was. It's as simple as that."

White-faced, she gathered up the whole bundle of papers and went into the bedroom with them.

CHAPTER XIV

SHE WAS still deep in them at eleven, and as she showed no sign of wanting to talk any more, or indeed of wanting me around at all, I said good night and took myself off to the guest room.

There, I tossed and turned for hours, wrestling with the ghastly syllogism she'd forced on me. "Fay was a murderess. Carol is exactly like her. Therefore Carol is a potential murderess."

The trouble was, I could find no flaw in it. I suppose

I never had really believed there'd been any appreciable difference between them. I'd tried to persuade myself when Fay had turned out to be bad, that was all. I'd heard them both on the subject too often, I'd watched them too closely, to have any real doubts. Carol's uncompromising insistence had merely confirmed what at heart I knew—they *had* been replicas.

That being so, the conclusion followed inescapably. I didn't want to accept it, but I couldn't reject it. I'd nothing to reject it *with*. I was only too aware that I'd never really got to know Carol. I'd been attracted by her, I'd been dazzled by her, I'd enjoyed every minute of our early days together—but the relationship had been a surface one. We'd thrown out no strong roots together. We'd had no problems, no worries—nothing to test us. In ten years' time I'd probably have been able to say with absolute certainty whether Carol was capable of being another Fay. At the moment I couldn't. So the syllogism stood—and I had to face it.

Thoughts which a few days before I'd have regarded as an impossible disloyalty now began to fill my mind. Wasn't Carol, I asked myself, in fact already far advanced along Fay's path—the path of the predatory adventuress? Hadn't she behaved like an adventuress from the beginning? I remembered the circumstances of our first meeting—the way her roving glance had taken in first my expensive car and then me, the way she'd smiled and said " Hallo," the way she'd hung about for me so that we could travel up the *sesselbahn* together, the interest she'd shown in my grand London flat and my pampered bachelor life and my excellent professional prospects, the readiness with which she'd agreed to meet me again once she'd sized the situation up. It had all seemed innocent

enough at the time—but not now. I recalled her earlier
background of poverty, her hard struggle on the stage,
her dreary Bayswater lodging—all things to escape
from. . . . It was curious, of course, that she hadn't
accepted more money from Arthur when she'd had the
chance—that didn't seem to fit. But she'd certainly done
very well out of me. In the past few months she'd had all
the luxury that any woman could want—and how she'd
revelled in it! Looked at objectively, she'd already proved
herself a highly successful gold-digger. After what had
happened, how could I blind myself to it?

Yet I was still in love with her—that was the fantastic
thing. If, as sense and logic told me, she was another
Fay in the making, I ought to have felt revulsion in her
presence. I ought to have recoiled from her physically.
But I didn't. I still wanted her. I'd seen Fay change
almost before my eyes from a charming girl to a clawing
harpy, and I was still crazily in love with her spit and
image! I writhed in torment. . . .

Very soon I was arguing with myself all over again. If
Carol *was* another Fay, I told myself, she must know very
well that Fay was guilty. Knowing it, shouldn't she have
been eager to co-operate with me in looking for differences
between them, instead of throwing their likeness in my
face? Wouldn't that have been the sensible, the most
promising course for her—to try and bolster my credulity?
After all, her material prospects—indeed, her whole
future—depended largely on her being able to maintain
her position as an acceptable wife in spite of what had
happened. If she could do that, she could count absolutely on a life of wealth and ease; she could hope to
emerge after a while from the public cloud that now
enveloped her; she could look forward to an assured and

enviable status—probably, in the fullness of time, to becoming Lady Renison. A glittering prospect by any gold-digger's standards! But if she failed to maintain her position, and we drifted into separation, she could count on nothing but an allowance. She'd be on her own again —and as the twin sister of a proved murderess, discarded for that reason by her husband, she'd be very much on her own. So why had she taken the line she had? By presenting a picture of herself that in the end I must find intolerable, she was surely taking a great risk of driving me from her—and losing most of what she'd struggled for. Was that the action of a gold-digger?

Then another thought struck me. Perhaps she'd realised that in the long run she hadn't a hope of presenting herself convincingly as being different from Fay. Perhaps she'd realised that whatever I might *want* to believe, the evident likeness would continue to haunt me, till finally I couldn't bear it any longer. If she *had* thought that, she was almost certainly right. . . . Perhaps she'd seen a slightly more hopeful prospect in standing pat on Fay's innocence—in maintaining, with all the fire and fervour she was capable of, that a mistake had been made. If she could only persuade me of that, her future would be safe. . . . But could she really think that it would be possible to persuade me, in face of all the evidence? Could she be so arrogantly confident of her power . . . ?

Well, events would show—and meanwhile I could get no further with the problem. I took four aspirins, and presently subsided into an uneasy doze.

Carol was as pale and heavy-eyed at breakfast as I was myself. I guessed she'd spent most of the night digesting the inquest report, which no doubt accounted for her much more subdued manner. That evidence would have subdued anyone. She was polite, and cold, and a million miles away from me. I decided to be polite and cold too.

As she poured coffee, I said, " Well—have you had any second thoughts? "

She didn't answer for a moment. Then she said, " I can see now *why* you believed it. . . . But *I* still don't, and I never will."

" You've decided to close your mind to the facts and rely on your sixth sense! "

" I suppose it must seem like that to you, though it's not entirely true. . . ."

" How isn't it true? "

Her face became very thoughtful and concentrated. " Well—even if Fay *had* meant to get rid of Arthur, which she didn't, I can't see things happening as they were supposed to have happened."

" What things? "

" The accident to the dinghy, for a start. Fay was very experienced with boats."

" But she wasn't in a normal state. She was probably in a desperate hurry, as Burns said, and panicked when she lost the oar."

" It would be very difficult to catch an anchor in the halter of a swim-suit—so high up."

" I don't see why. She'd have had to lift it to throw it overboard."

" A dinghy anchor's very light—only a few pounds. . . ."

I shrugged. " It must have happened, anyway. . . . What else? "

" Well, she undressed and left her clothes at the Point but she took her handbag to the island, or it wouldn't have been in the dinghy. She must have swum across holding it above the water. I'd have thought she would have left it with her clothes—it would have been quite safe."

" Don't women always hang on to their handbags? "

" They don't usually swim with them . . . ! Then there's a point about the insulin. Why would she have bothered to bring it away? She could have taken it out of its bag and loosened the top of the bottle and spilled it in the sand. It would still have looked like an accident. Then there'd have been no problem about someone having to go back with it later. . . . It would have been a better plan, don't you think? "

I could scarcely meet her eyes. Not only had she been through all the evidence in a purposefully systematic way, searching for little weaknesses that she could put to me —she was now showing, I realised, precisely the same subtle, tortuous mind as Fay would have needed to work out the murder plot!

I said, " Fay may not have wanted to touch the bottle. There'd have been a fingerprint danger."

" Oh—I see. . . ." She was silent for a moment. Then she said, " What about that note in her bag? Wouldn't you have expected her to destroy it? "

" I dare say she intended to," I said. " She'd have waited till she got home, though. She wouldn't have wanted to risk anyone finding the bits, and piecing them together."

Carol looked at me doubtfully. I thought she was going to pursue the point, but she didn't. Instead, she said, " Anyhow, the plot itself doesn't seem a very good one to me. According to the newspaper story, Fay and this man were expecting Arthur's death to be attributed to *two* accidents—first, his losing the insulin, and second, his not having made the dinghy properly secure, so that it drifted away. . . . Wouldn't that have been straining coincidence a bit? "

" I'm sure they'd have got away with it," I said.

" Well, perhaps. . . ." She paused again. " There's a point about the telephone call—several, in fact. If the man was around in the sandhills that day, as the police suggested, wouldn't he have *known* whether Fay had ' managed it ' or not . . . ? He wouldn't have had to ring up and ask."

" We don't know what his movements were," I said patiently. " He obviously wasn't around at the crucial time, or he'd have been able to rescue Fay. I should think he probably left the note in the early hours, while it was still dark, and kept right out of the way in daylight. It would have been the sensible thing to do."

" It seems very strange to me that he should have arranged to ring up that evening at all. He'd have known that Fay would have to give the alarm when Arthur didn't come back—so it was well on the cards there'd be people in the house. . . ."

" Perhaps she planned to give the alarm after he'd rung. We don't know what her plans were."

" That's the trouble—we know so little. . . . I wish I'd been at the inquest—there are so many questions. . . ."

" Franklin decided you weren't well enough to stand another shock," I said, " and I'm sure he was right. We did the best we could—it wasn't easy. . . ."

" Oh, I'm not really blaming you for that. . . ."

" As for asking questions, the man I got down from London did everything possible. . . . I dare say a few more points could have been raised, but what was the use? Nothing would have been changed. All these things you've mentioned are completely trifling, compared with the rest of the evidence."

" Well, I can't accept any of the evidence," Carol said stubbornly.

I sighed. " Not even that the insulin was found in Fay's handbag! "

" Oh, yes—but I don't believe she took it."

" Then who did? "

" Someone else, of course."

" And put it in her bag! "

" I suppose so."

I shook my head. " It's no use, Carol. . . . Can't you see that all the evidence goes together? The slit pocket, the insulin in the bag, the note, the telephone call. . . . If Fay didn't do it, the only possible explanation would be some colossal frame-up covering every detail—and that's beyond belief."

" Is it? The only thing that's beyond belief to me is that Fay had anything to do with it. Perhaps it *was* a frame-up. Perhaps that's why Fay had to have her ' accident '. . . . We know she was drowned—but how? The papers say there were bruises on her."

" The bruises were explained. . . . Carol, you're not putting this forward seriously? "

" I know Fay didn't do it. If a frame-up is the only alternative, then I believe in a frame-up. . . . Is it impossible? "

I sat thinking about it. Physically, it might have been done, I supposed. In favourable circumstances, the insulin could have been abstracted and the pocket slit before Fay's arrival. Fay *could* have been intercepted and held under water and drowned, the insulin and the note *could* have been planted in her bag, the boat accident *could* have been faked and the boat set adrift by the murderer. But the detailed planning would have been incredibly complicated, the hazards enormous. It wasn't, perhaps, absolutely impossible—but it was wildly improbable.

" Your hypothetical murderer would have had to know an awful lot about the set-up in Norfolk," I said.

" Of course."

" He'd have had to know about Arthur's diabetes."

" Everyone at Embery Staithe knew about that, so why shouldn't he? "

" He'd have had to know how vital the insulin was to Arthur—the effect of missing a dose—how long it would be before things started to happen. . . ."

" He could have read the subject up."

" H'm. . . . Tell me, is it your idea that Arthur's death would have been the main object of the exercise? —that your notional murderer would have disposed of Fay simply because a frame-up would have seemed the best way of safeguarding himself? "

" Well, that's one possibility. . . . Or the murderer might have *had* to kill Fay."

" Why? "

" To prevent her raising the alarm. He'd have known he couldn't count on Arthur's death taking place much under twenty-four hours—and Fay would have had people out there searching long before that."

" Not on the island," I said. " Not if the dinghy wasn't there. All that was gone into at the inquest, remember . . .? So it wouldn't have mattered if she had raised the alarm. Besides, Maureen would have raised it even if she hadn't."

" That's true. . . . All right, then, we come back to
your first suggestion. The murderer wanted to fix things
so there'd be no danger of anything being brought home
to him, and framing Fay was the way he chose."

" I don't see how he could possibly have been in a
position to choose it," I said. " How could he have been
sure that Fay would go out to join Arthur later that day,
and so deliver herself into his hands as a frame-up
instrument? Suppose she hadn't gone till the next
morning, which was quite a possibility—and then had
had someone with her, which was also likely. What
then? "

For a moment, Carol looked blank. Then she said,
without much assurance, " Well, perhaps he only decided
on his plan when he actually *saw* her going out. Perhaps
he was there already, and saw her approaching along the
sea wall, and that gave him the idea. . . ."

Again, I shook my head. " I'm quite sure no one
could have thought of a complicated plot like that on the
spur of the moment, let alone carried it out. . . . In any
case, I can't for the life of me see what your mythical
murderer would have gained by it all. If he'd wanted to
kill Arthur he could easily have knocked him on the
head some dark night on the sea wall—heaven knows
there were plenty of opportunities. It would have
been much less risky than what you're suggesting he
did."

Carol was silent.

" Anyway, there's still a big snag we haven't dealt
with. . . . What about the telephone call? "

Carol looked surprised. " I'd have thought that fitted
perfectly into the frame-up idea—like putting the note
into Fay's bag. The murderer would obviously have

wanted to strengthen the impression that Fay had a boy friend."

" Who would he have been hoping to convince? If he'd marooned Arthur and drowned Fay, he'd have expected the house to be empty. So why should he ring? "

" There was Maureen," Carol said doubtfully. " He might have known she'd be back."

" But the phone call only achieved the effect it did because he was able to say, ' Fay, darling, did you manage it? '—because of the confusion over the voices. He couldn't have hoped to work that with Maureen."

" Perhaps he knew *we* were there. Perhaps he'd seen us around."

" Well, we certainly didn't see him—I remember thinking at the time how utterly deserted the place was. There wasn't even a parked car."

" He could have been watching from behind the sea wall."

" What, for our totally unheralded arrival . . . ? No, it won't do. . . . Anyway, how would it have helped him even if he had known we were there? He couldn't have known you'd answer the phone. Suppose I'd answered it? "

" He could still have asked for Fay," Carol said, " and rung off without giving his name when he was told she wasn't there. That would have been quite suspicious enough. . . . Perhaps that was all he intended—and then, when I happened to answer the phone and the voice sounded the same, he took advantage. . . ."

" Well, it's possible," I said. " But as far as the frame-up idea as a whole is concerned, I'm afraid it seems quite preposterous to me. It would have been incredibly involved and dangerous—and pointless. It doesn't begin to take account of all the evidence, either. The night walks that Fay took on the sea wall—her insistence on going into Fairhaven that morning without any good reason—and then the determined way she went after Arthur. . . . Besides, why would anyone except Fay have *wanted* to kill Arthur? She would have got his money—but what would anyone else have got out of it? "

There was a little silence. Then Carol said, " Who gets Arthur's money now? "

" Why, his relatives, I suppose. The will he made leaving everything to Fay would have been void, since it was established that she died first."

" Arthur had only one relative that he knew of—a distant cousin."

" Oh, yes—I remember. . . . Then *he*'ll probably get it all."

Carol said, " Well, isn't *that* a strong motive—inheriting two hundred thousand pounds . . . ? Perhaps we've been on the wrong track all the time, thinking that Arthur was the main objective—perhaps Arthur and Fay were both killed because they were obstacles in the way of a fortune! That would account for the complicated frame-up plan, too—because unless everything had been neatly tied up, suspicion would obviously have fallen on whoever was going to benefit. . . . James, how do we know this distant cousin wasn't responsible for the whole thing? "

" It's the wildest notion," I said.

" How can you be sure, when we don't know who he is or what he's like or anything about him? "

" I tell you it's pure fantasy."

She got up and went over to the window. For a while she stood there, shoulders drooping, her pose infinitely weary and dejected. Then she said, " You know, James,

if you won't even consider any other possibilities, I can't
see that there's any hope for us at all. . . ."

I thought that was very unfair, after all the discussion
we'd had about her fanciful frame-up idea. " I'm ready
to *consider* anything," I said.

" But you're not. You say things are fantasy before
you've even looked into them. How can you *know* . . . ?
We could at least try to find out where this distant cousin
was at the time."

" It wouldn't do any good."

" It wouldn't do any harm—would it? What have we
got to lose? "

The answer to that, of course, was nothing.

CHAPTER XV

AN HOUR later I got on the phone to John Hamilton in
Norwich. He was very friendly and asked after Carol
and I told him she was much better. We chatted for a
moment or two. Then I said we had a notion to get in
touch with a cousin that Arthur had once spoken of and
wondered if by any chance he knew the man's name and
address.

" Well, that's odd," he said. " As a matter of fact,
I had a letter from him only yesterday. I'd heard about
him, too, and was going to advertise for him—but he
saved me the trouble. His name's Eric Templer, and the
address is St. Osyth's, The Green, Uxbridge, Middle-
sex."

I made a note of it. At least, I thought, Uxbridge

wasn't far away. The whole thing was quite preposterous, but if Carol insisted on seeing the man we could easily run over that morning and get it over.

" May I know what he said in the letter? " I asked.

" I don't see why not. . . . He said he'd read the report of the double tragedy in the papers, and noticed I was mentioned as Arthur's solicitor, and he was writing because he had an idea he was Arthur's only living relative."

" Did he say anything about himself? "

" Not a thing—it was quite a brief note."

I thanked him, and rang off, and went to tell Carol.

" Well—there you are! " she said. " He's so anxious to get hold of the money, he couldn't even wait to be traced."

" If he'd murdered Arthur and Fay for it," I said, " my guess is he *would* have waited .. . . He wouldn't have wanted to seem eager."

" I suppose that could be a clever double bluff."

I shook my head. " You're just spinning a web out of nothing. . . . Anyone who'd killed Arthur and Fay would have had to know their arrangements intimately—we agreed about that. . . . As far as we know, this man Templer never went near Arthur."

Carol frowned. " I seem to remember now that Arthur did once say his cousin had visited him. . . . It would have been before Fay married, of course, but it could have been a start. . . ."

I grunted. The recollection seemed to have come rather as an afterthought. I even wondered if Carol had made it up.

" He'd have seen at once that there was money about," she went on. " And Arthur would have been sure to tell him about his diabetes and the insulin, because he told everyone—so that could have suggested the method. ... He could have gone on turning it over in his mind, wanting to do it, but not sure he could get away with it because of his obvious motive—and then when Fay came on the scene he could have had his frame-up idea and decided it was safe to go ahead. ... He could have paid secret visits to Norfolk, and kept watch, and got to know the ground—it would have meant a lot of effort, but it would have seemed well worth while for all that money. A young, active man would have thought nothing of it. ...."

For a fleeting moment, I could almost believe that her idea wasn't as irrational as I'd thought. There was no doubt she had a real talent for building up a persuasive picture. After all, I told myself, if Arthur and Fay *had* died in any way but the one the coroner's court had decided, the true explanation was bound to seem pretty unlikely to start with. ... And it wouldn't be the first time in history that one cousin had killed another for an inheritance. ...

Then sanity returned. I was just deluding myself, of course. There wasn't a hope.

" Well, let's go and get it over," I said. " Shall I see if he's on the telephone—perhaps we ought to let him know we're coming."

" Won't that put him on his guard? "

I shrugged. " If he had a double murder on his mind I should think he'd be on his guard in any case! But just as you like. ... What are you proposing to say to him—' Where were you on the night of the crime? ' "

Carol wasn't to be put off. " If he had nothing to do with it," she said, " we ought to be able to find out where he was quite easily in the ordinary course of conversation. If he's at all cagy, or we don't believe what he says, we'll have to check with other people. If he was away at all, he must have been away for several days, so the tradesmen will probably know. . . ." There was a glint in her eye. " I'm quite sure there's *something* odd about him. If he hasn't got anything to hide, and he knows he's Arthur's only surviving relative, and he read about the tragedy in the papers, how was it he didn't show up at the inquest or the funeral! "

We reached Uxbridge well before lunch and had no difficulty in finding The Green. It was a quiet and charming spot, an oasis in suburbia. Behind a sweep of well-kept lawn there was a terrace of mellow old houses with quaint chimneys, all beautifully looked after. St. Osyth's, it appeared, was the name of the terrace—the houses themselves had numbers, but no names. We didn't know Templer's number, but an old man was crossing the lawn as though he belonged there and we walked over to him. He had white hair and a thin, frail body, and was leaning heavily on a rubber-tipped stick.

" Excuse me," I said, " but can you tell me where I can find Mr. Eric Templer? "

The old man looked at me in surprise. " Why, yes," he said. " I'm Eric Templer."

CHAPTER XVI

As we got back into the car twenty minutes later, Carol said, "How were we to know he was Arthur's *second* cousin? Or that St. Osyth's was an Old Men's Home?" Her exasperation sounded genuine—but I couldn't be sure.

I gave a little nod of agreement. The episode would have been laughable if our whole situation hadn't been so grim. As it was, I couldn't raise a smile.

"I wonder what he'll do with all the money?" Carol said.

"Nothing for very long, by the look of him." The old man had been alert enough mentally—he'd remembered very well his one brief call on Arthur five years before when he'd been staying at Cromer and had dropped in at Embery Staithe out of curiosity—but physically he'd appeared very feeble. Even the considerable comforts of St. Osyth's—which was no almshouse, but a quiet haven for elderly gentlemen of moderate means—seemed unlikely to keep him going much longer.

"You don't think," Carol said, "that perhaps *he* might have a relative—a much younger one—someone who knew the money would come to him when the old man died?"

"And who murdered Arthur and Fay because of it? No, I don't. . . . Heavens, how complicated can you get?"

There was silence for a while. Then Carol said, "Well,

if Arthur wasn't murdered for his money there must have been some other reason. Something in his life that we don't know about. If we search long enough, perhaps we'll be able to find out what it was. . . ." Far from being put off by the fiasco of the morning, her attitude seemed to have hardened.

I said, " Well, *I* certainly can't imagine any reason. From what I saw of him he was a most inoffensive chap —quiet, retiring, gentle, long-suffering. . . . Not at all the sort to get murdered. Apart from his diabetes, and the business with Fay at the end, I'd have said his life was very ordinary."

Carol appeared to consider that. " We don't really know much about his life, do we? Not the earlier part. We know he was at Cambridge, and we know he had a farm—and that's about all. Except, of course . . ." She broke off, looking at me intently. " Would you call it ordinary for your wife to be drowned on her honeymoon? "

" Well, no—of course not . . . But it's hardly a reason for murder, is it? For compassion, rather—just the opposite."

" All the same, it *was* an extraordinary incident—and if we're going to search we've got to start somewhere."

I stared at her. " You mean you seriously intend to go back over Arthur's past looking for possible grounds for murder? "

" Yes," she said. " And to begin with I'd like to know more about his first marriage. That accident must have been a tremendous thing in his life. . . . You know, it's curious that *both* his wives were drowned."

That jolted me. For a moment I had a grotesque vision of Arthur doing a sort of " brides-in-the-bath "

act and finally staging his own elaborate suicide. . . .
But naturally it didn't make any sense.

"Just a coincidence," I said.

"I suppose so. . . . Anyway, how can we find out
about Arthur's first marriage?"

"I expect we could get some information at Somerset
House, if you're absolutely set on it."

"I *would* like to. . . . Can we go this afternoon?"

The "we" wasn't lost on me. She was dragging me
deeper and deeper into this fatuous investigation. She
was deliberately making me a part of it. But what could
I do?

"All right," I said, "we'll go this afternoon."

We had no difficulty in getting the bare details of the
marriage—the facts that appeared on the certificate.
The girl's name had been Veronica Pashley. She'd been
a secretary, aged twenty-two, and had lived in Kensington.
The marriage had taken place at a church there on 7th
April, 1946. The girl's father had been Ernest John
Pashley, a builder. Arthur's father was entered as
George Edward Ramsden, manufacturer. I copied the
particulars into my diary.

"Well—now what?" I asked, as we left the building.

Carol looked at me thoughtfully. "James—if a girl
was drowned on her honeymoon wouldn't there be something about it in the newspapers at the time?"

"I should think there might be," I said.

"Well, we know when it happened. . . . Is there anywhere we could look at old newspapers?"

"There's the British Museum. . . . They've a place
out at Hendon where they keep files from the year dot."

"Can anyone go there?"

"You have to get a ticket, but you can get one on the spot for a short-term bit of investigation."

She took my arm. It was the first affectionate gesture she'd made for a long time—my reward, no doubt, for being co-operative. "Come on, then," she said.

The popular papers seemed the best bet, so we asked for the files of the *Mail* and the *Express*, for April 1946. It took a little time to get them up, but once we'd got them we didn't have to search long. As I turned the pages of the *Mail* for the 11th, my eye was caught by a familiar face. It was a picture of Arthur Ramsden, looking appreciably younger than when I'd known him, but quite unmistakable. A photograph of a good-looking girl was inset in the paragraph accompanying the picture. I called Carol from the other side of the table, and we read through the item together. It said:

"The honeymoon of a young London couple ended tragically in the Scilly Isles yesterday when Veronica Ramsden, 22, the four-day-old bride of Arthur Ramsden, of Hampstead, was drowned after falling from a cliff.

"The Ramsdens were exploring the top of the cliff above a cove called Hell's Mouth when Mrs. Ramsden slipped and fell headlong into the sea. Mr. Ramsden rushed down to the beach and, though unable to swim, at once plunged into the water in a desperate effort to save his wife. The sea was very rough at the time and before he could reach her she was swept away. When Mr. Ramsden finally struggled ashore he was in an exhausted condition. The body of Mrs. Ramsden has not yet been recovered.

"Mr. Ramsden, a temporary civil servant at the Ministry of Agriculture, is the son of Mr. George Ramsden, chairman of Joseph Grantley Ltd., the agricultural machinery manufacturers. Mrs. Ramsden was the only daughter of Mr. and Mrs. Ernest Pashley, of Old Stones, Bridport."

So that was how it had happened. Even though it was so long ago, even though Arthur was dead, it was impossible to read the stark account without horror and pity. Arthur certainly had been an unlucky man. . . .

I turned up the succeeding issues of the paper to see if there'd been a follow-up to the story. In the issue of the 12th I found a brief item, saying that Mrs. Ramsden's body had been washed ashore. A couple of days later there was a short report of the inquest, which had followed the normal pattern. The verdict had been "Accidental death" and the coroner had commended Arthur for his rescue attempt and offered his sympathy.

Carol copied all the names and addresses into a notebook and closed the file. "Well, there isn't much there, is there?" she said.

"What did you expect?"

"I didn't expect anything. I'm looking—that's all. This is only the beginning. . . ."

"You mean to go on searching?"

"Yes," she said, "and I'd like you to help me. . . . If you won't, I'll just have to go ahead on my own."

CHAPTER XVII

WHEN YOU'VE LOST hope you'll try almost anything—and that was the state I was in. I couldn't doubt that unless something pretty dramatic turned up to change the situation, my marriage to Carol was headed for the rocks. Our suspended relationship was already more like domestic cold war than marriage, and I knew that a final, shattering flare-up might occur at any moment. I couldn't let that happen without exhausting every possibility first. So, though I hadn't the slightest expectation that any good would come of it, and though I was as distrustful as ever of her motives, I decided to help Carol with her self-imposed piece of research. There was still, I told myself, the outside chance that she was genuine, that she really believed she might find something, that she was trying to save our marriage because she was fond of me and not for what it gave her. If, on the other hand, her only purpose was to dredge up raw material for a seductive new theory, it would fail, and we'd be no worse off. I still had nothing to lose. That evening I told her that I was completely at her disposal. . . . There were tears in her eyes as she thanked me.

During the next few days we systematically turned back the pages of Arthur Ramsden's life in an attempt to find out why anyone could have wanted to kill him. It was hard going to start with because we knew so little about him, but the facts we'd gleaned from the newspaper paragraph helped quite a bit and one thing led to another.

I used my now rather uncertain status at the F.O. quite shamelessly to get us the entrées we needed. We talked to tutors and lecturers at Cambridge, to civil servants who'd known Arthur in the old days at the Ministry of Agriculture, and to numerous employees at Grantley's. We discovered from John Hamilton the address of the farm that Arthur had owned in Devonshire, and travelled down there and interviewed several of his former neighbours. On the way back we stopped at Bridport and found Veronica Pashley's mother, now a widow, still living at Old Stones, and talked to her. It was an arduous and often delicate investigation, with constant embarrassments, because of course everyone knew about the Norfolk case and being Fay's sister wasn't exactly a commendation. Sometimes, to get our questions answered at all, we had to drop hints that there might be more in the case than was known about, which usually aroused interest, if also a good deal of scepticism. Sometimes, Carol's evident grief over the tragedy gained sympathy for her, and people were kind. When her natural appeal failed, I usually managed to achieve our ends by quiet diplomacy on my own. At the end of a week of unremitting questioning I felt I knew pretty well everything about Arthur's life that there was to be known. And, of course, none of it helped.

Broadly, the picture was this. At Cambridge, Arthur had been a diligent and—within his own hard-working circle—a quite popular student. He had graduated with honours in agriculture and kindred subjects shortly after the beginning of World War II. He had taken a job for a few months at his father's works and had then moved to the Ministry of Agriculture, where as a civil servant he was exempt from the call-up and had served until the

end of hostilities. At the Ministry he'd proved a con-
scientious and promising young administrator, and he
was still remembered there as a rather friendly person.
After the war he'd returned for a short time to Grantley's.
In 1946 he'd married Veronica Pashley, who by all
accounts had been an unusually charming girl, and the
honeymoon tragedy had followed. His health had been
undermined by the shock and he'd been sent on a world
cruise by his father, who thought the world of him, in the
hope that new sights would take his mind off things. On
his return, physically restored, the old man had bought
a farm for him on the outskirts of Dartmoor. It had been
a high moorland farm in poor condition, deliberately
chosen on that account. Arthur had thrown himself
into the work of reclamation with feverish energy and in
the seven years he'd been there he'd built it up into a
flourishing place. Once at the farm, he'd rarely left it.
His father had visited him regularly until his death in
1948, but otherwise Arthur had led a very self-contained
life, making few friends and for weeks on end living almost
like a recluse. He'd stayed at the farm until 1954, when
he'd developed diabetes, and he'd then sold up and
moved to Norfolk.

Though there were still a few periods of his life that
we hadn't been able to investigate—notably the time of
the world cruise—we'd done, on the whole, a very
thorough job. At every stage of the inquiry we'd probed
deeply for the slightest hint of trouble—but there simply
wasn't any. If Arthur had made few friends, he seemed
not to have made any enemies, either. No one had
spoken about him with great affection, probably because
of the pronounced misanthropic streak which had developed after his first wife's death—but no one had had

anything to say against him. Indeed, we'd found a great deal of respect for his hard work and technical achievements. Between Veronica Pashley and Fay there seemed to have been no women in his life at all. He'd been law-abiding and temperate, and there'd been no breath of scandal of any sort. If anyone had had a reason for murdering him, we had signally failed to find it. Even Carol, with her purposeful imagination, hadn't been able to think of anything.

She was rather quiet the night we returned to the flat but, to my surprise, not wholly despondent. Faith—or was it some secret new ploy?—still buoyed her up. Personally I felt worn out and utterly depressed by the futile search. " It's like the old definition of metaphysics," I said.

" What's that? " Carol asked.

" A blind man searching in a dark room for a black cat that isn't there! "

" But it *is* there," she said firmly. " It *must* be."

CHAPTER XVIII

NEXT MORNING she suddenly decided that she'd like to go to Norfolk again. There was still one period of Arthur's life, she pointed out, that we were in a position to cover and hadn't—the five years he'd spent at Embery Staithe before he'd met Fay. Since it was the most recent period, it might well be the crucial one. She knew the name of the housekeeper who'd looked after Arthur—a Mrs. Pearce, who now lived at Fairhaven—and she'd like to talk to her. Afterwards we could go back to the house on the creek and see if we could discover anything helpful among Arthur's effects.

I couldn't have been less enthusiastic. We were already familiar with the pattern of Arthur's life in Norfolk, and I doubted if we should learn anything fresh. It seemed very unlikely that he would have kept evidence of trouble in a house that he shared with Fay. Apart from that, I hated the idea of Carol returning so soon to the scene of the tragedy and stirring up poignant memories. It was a protective attitude that didn't square at all with my vigorous suspicions of her, but I couldn't help it. It any case, it made no difference. Carol was obviously determined to go, and I knew she'd go by herself if necessary. So after breakfast I got the car out and we drove once more to Norfolk, with an overnight bag in the boot in case we couldn't get back that day.

We found Mrs. Pearce in a neat waterfront cottage on the fringe of Fairhaven. She was a small, active woman of sixty or so, with a brisk, efficient manner. At first she seemed inclined to resent Carol's visit, which was hardly surprising, but she thawed out in the end and we had a long talk. As I'd foreseen, it got us nowhere. Arthur's life, we gathered, had been completely smooth and trouble-free during those five years. Nothing in the least disturbing had ever happened. Occasionally he might have been a bit moody, but then who wasn't? Mostly he'd been rather cheerful. As an employer he'd always been kind and considerate. . . . It was rather like one of those appreciations that friends of the deceased contribute to *The Times*. If Mrs. Pearce *had* known anything sinister, I was sure she wouldn't have told us. But I was equally sure she'd nothing to tell.

We lunched in a restaurant in Fairhaven—and got

some pretty curious stares. Carol seemed scarcely to notice, but I felt distinctly uncomfortable. Immediately after lunch we drove on to Embery Staithe. I collected the house key from the village shop and we let ourselves in. The place was just as we'd left it ten days before— no one had been there. To me it was full of ghosts, but once again Carol seemed quite indifferent to atmosphere —she was bent on her search, and was already beginning to rummage among Arthur's things. Presently I joined her.

The search turned out to be very straightforward. Arthur had been a methodical man, and most of his personal effects and papers were neatly arranged in the room he'd used as a study. There were several files of correspondence and receipts, which we divided between us and ploughed steadily through. Carol was tense with concentration, but I soon found my attention wandering, for there was nothing in the least illuminating. I glanced through Arthur's passport, which was newish and showed only two trips abroad—a visit to France three years earlier, and a fortnight in the Canaries, where he'd spent his honeymoon with Fay. There were no property deeds or investment documents or insurance policies—these, no doubt, were lodged with his bank or with Hamilton. Carol found his birth certificate, which showed he'd been born in Luton in 1920; and his two marriage certificates. There was a whole drawerful of photographs he'd taken himself, some of them loose and some of them in albums. We went through them carefully, but there was nothing of special interest to us. The only framed photograph was a cabinet portrait of Fay that stood on his desk.

Carol suddenly said, " James, do you realise there isn't a photograph of his first wife anywhere? "

I shrugged. "That's not very surprising, is it? He was a man of sensibility."

"Oh, I don't mean I'd expect to see one hanging on the wall—but surely he'd have kept a picture of her some-where—privately?"

"His memories must have been dreadful," I said. "Probably he just wanted to forget. Very natural, in the circumstances."

"*I* don't think it's natural. . . . I can't believe a man would get rid of *every* picture of a girl he'd loved, just because the thing had ended in a tragic accident. He'd put them aside—he'd start life again—but they'd be there. . . . Forgotten relics, if you like—but he'd have to be an extraordinary man to throw them on the fire."

I said, "H'm." It sounded to me as though Carol were trying to start another of her hares.

I began to examine the books round the walls. There were a lot of them, covering a wide range of subjects—photography, ornithology, diseases of the pancreas, quite a bit of psychology. But there was nothing specially striking, and again I found my attention wandering. While Carol continued to pry in the recesses of Arthur's desk I took a look in the cupboard annexe which he'd evidently used as a dark room, and climbed to the loft, and generally went through the rest of the house. When I'd finished, I was still no wiser. The house hadn't told us a thing. From all our ransacking investigations, Arthur had emerged as an intelligent, sensitive, cultured man, who'd led a full and interesting life with a wife to whom he'd been uncommonly attached. And we'd known all that before.

I returned to the study to find Carol poring over a slim,

black-bound folder. "James," she said, "do come and look at this. . . ."

"What is it?" I asked.

"Arthur's bank statement. . . . Just look at these amounts he drew in cash. I make it more than two thousand pounds in the last four months."

"Really . . . ?" That *was* intriguing. I joined her at the table and she showed me the items. Four cheques had been drawn to "self" at intervals of four or five weeks, each being a little larger than the last. For a moment I simply couldn't imagine why Arthur would have needed all that cash. . . . Then I suddenly remembered.

"Of course—it would have been for the sales he attended. People often take cash to sales."

"Could he really have spent all that?"

"Easily, I should think. . . . Some of the pieces here are very choice, you know."

"But—four sales in four months. Isn't that rather a lot?"

"Not for an enthusiast. . . ."

Carol was slowly turning back the pages of the statement, examining the earlier items. "He doesn't seem to have drawn much cash before April—but he must have gone to sales before then."

"Perhaps they were a different sort of sale," I said. "I imagine you'd pay by cheque at one of the big London places—and perhaps find cash more convenient at a country house. . . ." Actually, I didn't know much about it. "What are you driving at?"

"Well—I was thinking . . . James, you don't suppose someone could have been *blackmailing* him, do you?"

"I shouldn't think so for a moment."

" The amounts do go up each time—and that's just what you'd expect with blackmail."

" Pure chance," I said. " Anyway, if Arthur had drawn out this money to make blackmail payments, he'd hardly have left his bank statements lying about—perhaps for Fay to see. . . . He'd have destroyed them."

Carol looked unconvinced. " If he'd made a habit of keeping them before, it might have seemed odd if he'd suddenly started to destroy them. . . . And he could always have *said* it was for sales, if Fay had got to know. . . ."

" It must have been for sales," I said. " What could he have been blackmailed about? "

" There might have been something. . . ."

" Well, we've been through his life with a fine comb, and there certainly wasn't a hint of anything."

" He *behaved* like a man who was being blackmailed," Carol said. " It would account for his moodiness—his fits of depression. . . ."

" So would doubts about Fay's fidelity! "

She ignored that. " And it would explain those night walks along the sea wall. . . . When he *met* someone . . . ! The other person who was moving about—remember? "

" That was Fay's version."

" I know—and it's the version I believe. . . ."

" Then I suppose you also believe her story that she saw Arthur *kneeling* one night? "

" Yes. . . ."

" How does that fit in with your blackmail idea? What would he have been kneeling for? "

She looked at me with the fixed stare of someone who was thinking hard. I felt sure she'd come up with something in the end—and she did!

" Perhaps he was hiding the money—burying it. . . ."

" Why would he do that if he'd gone to meet a black-mailer with it? "

" Well—he might not have been actually *meeting* the blackmailer," she said. " After all, it was in quite a different place that Fay thought she heard someone else. . . . Perhaps Arthur had been told where to put the money, and the blackmailer was going to collect it afterwards. Perhaps Arthur didn't even know who the blackmailer was—that does happen, doesn't it . . . ? The man could have done everything on the telephone—it would have been much safer for him that way. . . ."

I checked the stream of fantasy. " Tell me one thing," I said. " Just one thing."

" Well? "

" Even if Arthur was being blackmailed, how would it help *you*? Have you ever heard of a blackmailer murdering his victim? That really would be killing the goose. . . . Isn't it always the other way round? "

Carol suddenly looked quite deflated. " Yes—I suppose it is," she said.

It was a retreat—for the moment. I wondered how much farther the next jump would take her!

CHAPTER XIX

THE SEARCH and the argument had used up the afternoon and an early October dusk wasn't far away. We were both tired after our big day and there seemed no point in driving back to London in the dark when we could get a bath, a good meal and a bed within a stone's throw of us. I took the key back to the shop and we went along to the hotel. I doubted if we'd be terribly welcome visitors there, but it was only for a night. Actually, the receptionist did look a bit startled at first, but she soon recovered and booked us in without fuss.

It was an unusual hotel—perhaps because it catered so much for eccentric people like bird-watchers and dinghy-sailors. The porter-cum-handyman talked with a B.B.C. accent and might well have been the manager. The Italian girls who made up the staff were constantly breaking into gales of laughter. The service, though willing, was erratic. But the rooms were excellent, and the bath water piping hot. I lay and soaked for half an hour, washing away the grime of Arthur's papers, and then went and had a long drink while Carol finished dressing. The strain of being constantly with her in an atmosphere of dispute and distrust was beginning to tell, and it was a relief to relax under a neutral roof—on my own. Carol seemed to share my feelings, for after dinner she rather pointedly retired to the farthest corner of the lounge and buried herself in a magazine that I couldn't believe she was reading. I had a few more drinks in the bar and then went out for a stroll. There was a notice on the door, characteristic of the place, asking the last person in at night to lock up. I wondered how anyone could know.

Carol was still very preoccupied in the morning. She showed no sign of being in a hurry to leave, and I didn't rush her. I remembered that I'd meant to ring up John Hamilton about a few outstanding matters, and decided I might as well do it from there. It turned out he had some things he wanted to discuss, too, and he suggested I should go over to Norwich. Carol was quite willing for me to go, but she said she was feeling rather tired and would sooner stay behind and spend the morning quietly by the creek. She would see me at lunch, she said. That was all right with me, and presently I went off alone.

I had about an hour with Hamilton, discussing various minor points to do with Arthur's estate and Fay's bits of property. He asked me if we'd seen Eric Templer and I told him about our visit—without disclosing the real reason for it. He didn't ask me what we were doing in Norfolk, and I didn't tell him. I left him soon after twelve and drove back to Embery Staithe at a leisurely pace.

There was no sign of Carol at the hotel when I got there just before one. I asked the porter if he'd seen her go out and he said, yes, at about eleven. He thought she'd gone for a walk, but he hadn't noticed which direction she'd taken. I looked along the sea wall, but it was deserted right to the sandbanks. I walked along to the house on the off-chance that she'd gone back there, but the place was shut up. I went into the village and looked along the main road both ways, but it was empty.

I couldn't think where she could have gone to. She'd said she was tired—surely she wouldn't have been walking for two hours. In any case she should have been back for lunch by now—or at least visible. . . . Suddenly I began to feel uneasy. There was something unpleasantly familiar about this situation. Arthur had disappeared, Fay had disappeared—and now Carol was missing. . . . I didn't really believe there could be any connection, but there'd been so much mischief. . . . I told myself the best thing I could do was to go into the bar and wait for her there, but I didn't. Instead I went down to the boat yard to see if by any chance she'd taken a dinghy out.

She hadn't. I started to walk back along the creek. At that moment the bus from Fairhaven pulled up in the main road fifty yards away—and Carol got out. She saw me and waved and came hurrying down to the creek with an unaccustomedly buoyant step. I was relieved that she'd turned up, but I also felt rather annoyed.

"What on earth have you been up to?" I asked, as she joined me. "I thought you were going to rest this morning."

"Let's go to our room," she said, "we can talk better there." Her face wore a look of flushed excitement—there was obviously something in the wind. She turned and walked rapidly towards the hotel. I followed her up to the bedroom and shut the door.

"All right," I said, "let's have it!"

"I think I've worked out a reason why a blackmailer might decide to kill his victim."

So she was still harping on her blackmailer! I said, "Oh?" without enthusiasm. I'd expected something more dramatic.

"Yes," she said eagerly. "Look, James—suppose that what we imagined about him being just a telephone voice was right—that his identity wasn't known to his victim. Suppose he *had* given his instructions about the money on the phone, and had planned to collect it only after his victim had departed. . . . Without ever showing himself. . . . He'd feel pretty safe, wouldn't he?"

"He'd feel fairly safe, I dare say."

"As safe as a blackmailer could, anyway. . . . He'd know that even if his victim went to the police, they'd have great difficulty in finding out who he was. They'd have to lie in wait for him where the money was hidden

—they'd have to stage some sort of ambush—and in open country that would be a very hard thing to do without the preparations becoming obvious. . . . I think he'd be in a very strong position."

" Well? "

" Well—now suppose that by some chance the victim was able to discover who the blackmailer was—that would alter everything, wouldn't it? Once the police knew his identity, they'd be able to keep track of him without his knowledge, check his phone calls, gather their evidence— and then pounce. . . . Wouldn't they? "

" I should think so."

" And what sort of sentence would a man get if he were convicted of blackmail? "

" Oh—up to seven years, in a bad case."

" There you are, then. If the blackmailer was a very ruthless man, and he knew his identity had been discovered, he might well decide to kill his victim before he could go to the police, rather than risk seven years."

" M'm . . ." She'd reached her objective, but I wasn't impressed by her argument. " It would be a very drastic step—and frankly I can't believe that the difference in danger in the two cases would be enough to make him take it. . . . An ambush would be tricky, I agree, but the police are pretty smart and he'd know they would probably get him once they'd been told about him, whether they knew his identity or not. A blackmailer's only real safe- guard is the reluctance of the victim to go to the police —and if a man hadn't had the guts to do it in the one case, he wouldn't be likely to in the other. That's how I see it, anyway. As far as I'm concerned I'm afraid you've had an inventive morning for nothing."

" But it isn't entirely invention," she said.

I stared at her.

"I've been very busy since you left, James. . . . Actually, I wasn't thinking along these lines at all to begin with, it just came to me by chance. I started out with quite another thought in my mind—one that wouldn't have appealed to you at all. Simply that everything Fay said was the literal truth. Including the fact that she had important business in Fairhaven that Saturday morning."

"But she didn't—we know that."

"I decided she must have—and I started wondering again what it could be. . . . Well, it obviously wasn't the ham and the tea, because she could have got those here —so there was only one thing left. It *had* to be those photographs."

"I looked at them," I said. "There wasn't a thing. . . ."

"Well, I thought I'd take another look. I remembered noticing them at the house yesterday—I suppose the police sent them back—so I collected the key and went and got them. . . ." She opened her bag and took out the yellow packet and spread the prints and negatives out on the bed.

I examined them again, more closely this time. I thought perhaps I might have missed something to do with the negatives, so I paired them up with the pictures, but they all matched. The only prints I lingered over at all were the two flashlight interiors, which I thought were of one of the bedrooms at the house. They had both been taken from almost the same position, which seemed rather a waste of film. And they were very dull—it wasn't as though there'd been anyone *in* the room. They might have meant something to Arthur technically, I supposed—but they certainly meant nothing to me.

" No," I said finally. " As far as I can see there's nothing here of any interest at all."

" That's exactly the point," Carol said.

" What do you mean? "

" How many films are there in a roll, James? "

I ran my eye quickly over the prints. They often came in eights, but I could see more than eight. " In this case, twelve, I should think. . . ."

" Well," Carol said, " there are only eleven here! "

CHAPTER XX

AT FIRST I thought she'd rather overplayed the curtain line she'd been so carefully working up to.

" Probably one of the pictures failed to come out," I said. " It could be as simple as that."

Carol shook her head. " That occurred to me, too. . . . It didn't seem very likely, because you usually get all the negatives back even if they're no good, but I thought I'd better make sure. That's why I went into Fairhaven this morning. The man at the shop remembered Fay calling, and he remembered he'd charged her for twelve prints. He was quite certain about it. So one negative and one print are definitely missing."

" Extraordinary ! I suppose he couldn't remember anything about them? "

" No—I asked him, of course, but he hadn't any idea at all. The young man who does the developing and printing came and looked at the prints, but he couldn't help either. He said so many films go through his hands that he hardly gives them a glance."

" Where have we got to, then? "

" Well, I think we've got quite a long way. Obviously, it was the missing photograph that was important to Fay. If it was so important—and secret—that she made a special journey to get it without mentioning it to anyone, I'm sure it must have been a picture she'd taken herself. And someone else was so concerned about it that he stole it from her—and murdered her. That all adds up to something, don't you think? "

" You're suggesting that she took a photograph of your notional blackmailer! "

" That's what it looks like to me. She could have taken it that last time she and Arthur were out late—two nights before the murder."

" What—in the dark? "

" She could have taken a flashlight picture."

" Heavens," I said, " you're not seriously suggesting that she stalked her quarry along the sea wall with an armful of apparatus? "

" No, I don't think that would have been very practical . . . she could have used the dinghy, though."

" The dinghy! "

"I think that's what she must have done. A spent flashbulb was found in the bottom—remember? And I never heard of Arthur taking flashlight pictures from the boat. None of the pictures he ever showed us were that sort."

" I bet the bulb was Arthur's, all the same," I said. " Why would Fay have thrown it there? Once she'd taken her picture, she'd have cleared off—she wouldn't have stopped to take the bulb out of the camera."

" She might have been hoping for a second picture."

" She could only have been hoping for a second one,"

I pointed out, " if she'd had another exposure available
—and with the missing one, all twelve are accounted for.
. . . You're not suggesting she hoped the blackmailer
would wait while she changed the roll! "

Carol frowned. Once more she studied the prints on
the bed. Then her face cleared. " *I've* got it . . . ! "

" Well? "

" Don't you see?—those two indoor pictures that
seemed so pointless. . . . They're of Fay's bedroom. She
had got some exposures left—two. And she used them up
in her room to finish the roll. She wouldn't have wanted
to take it to the shop partly unexposed, in case someone wondered why she was in such a hurry and took
too much interest. . . . So that's one more thing that
fits."

It was ingenious, even satisfying—and yet I wondered.
. . . Carol was like Procrustes, she made everything fit!

" Well," I said, " I find it all very hard to imagine. It
sounds a most unlikely sort of enterprise. At the most,
Fay could only have *guessed* there might be a blackmailer. . . ."

" She'd have had strong grounds for her guess," Carol
said. " I know she didn't think of it to start with, but it
would have been an obvious possibility on the evidence—
the secret walks, and Arthur being so angry when he was
tackled about them, and his strange behaviour in the
sand when he could have been hiding something—and, of
course, the other person she heard moving around there.
. . . Perhaps even the bank statement—who knows? "

" Well—maybe. . . . But how could she have possibly
hoped to find anyone in a dinghy? "

" I think that's simple enough. . . . She knew the
place where Arthur had been kneeling—where, on the

blackmail theory, he'd been accustomed to leave the
money. So all she had to do was anchor off there and
wait for the blackmailer to collect it. . . . I know it must
seem almost incredible to you that Fay could have gone
off alone in a dinghy at night to hunt a blackmailer she
wasn't even sure existed—but she was so worried when
she talked to me that last time that I know she'd have
done *anything* to get to the bottom of Arthur's extraordinary behaviour. . . . She was a *very* determined
person."

Yes, I thought grimly, like her sister! I hadn't any
doubts at all about Fay's determination—only a still
unshaken certainty about how she'd used it.

" What you've got to remember," Carol went on, " is
that it would have been quite natural for her to go in the
dinghy. She felt at home in it, and she knew the creek
like the back of her hand, and it would all have seemed
much easier to her than following people in the dark on
foot. Much safer, too. . . . She could have got close in
to the shore and taken her photograph without any risk
to herself. She might easily have got a perfect picture of
the man—absolutely red-handed. . . ."

I pondered. " That would have been on the Thursday
night, wouldn't it . . . ? When did Fay take her photographs to be developed—do we know? "

" Yes, it was first thing on the Friday morning—I asked
at the shop. She was there almost as soon as it opened—
she obviously couldn't wait a minute. Which is exactly
what you'd expect."

" She could have developed them herself—I'm sure
she knew how to. . . ."

" Not with Arthur around."

" She could have told him what she'd done. If there's

anything in your theory, that's obviously what she was going to do when she rushed round to the Point on the Saturday morning—so why not do it right away? "

" For one thing, because she wouldn't have known for certain how the picture was going to come out. After the rows they'd had, she'd probably have preferred to wait till she was sure of her evidence. I know *I* would."

I nodded. That made sense all right. . . . Carol's theory was actually standing up to fire pretty well. . . . Then, as I continued to turn it over in my mind, a new and powerful objection occurred to me.

" Look," I said, " I can see, up to a point, that this hypothetical blackmailer of yours might have felt he had to do something drastic if his photograph had been taken —but wouldn't it have been enough for him to dispose of Fay, while she was on her way to show the picture to Arthur? Once she was dead, and he'd collected the print and the negative from her bag, he'd have been all right. Why kill Arthur, too? Why involve himself in all these complications? "

Carol considered that for a while. " Well—I can think of one possible explanation. . . . He might have thought that Arthur wouldn't believe in the genuineness of Fay's accident. Arthur would have had every reason to wonder —he knew there was a tough character around, he knew Fay had been wandering about at night looking into things. . . . He'd probably have discovered, too, that there were only eleven photographs in the packet in Fay's bag, instead of the usual twelve, and that would have set him thinking. . . ."

" Why couldn't your blackmailer have removed *all* the photographs—the whole packet? "

" That would have been even more dangerous. Someone would have been sure to learn that Fay had collected photographs that morning—and if there'd been no trace of them, Arthur would have been suspicious at once. . . . Actually, I wouldn't be surprised if the blackmailer decided from the beginning that he couldn't safely kill one without the other—they both knew too much to believe in accidents."

"Well," I said, "it's all very fascinating. . . ."

Carol looked at me sadly. "It would be," she said, "if Fay and Arthur weren't dead. . . ."

CHAPTER XXI

I SAT quietly thinking things over while she made herself ready for lunch. There was no doubt it was quite a theory she'd conjured up from so little, and while I didn't for a moment believe in it I couldn't dismiss it out of hand. I still thought it most unlikely that a blackmailer would resort to murder simply because his identity was about to become known to his victim—but perhaps it wasn't absolutely impossible. I still thought it unlikely that he'd have committed two murders when one would have done —but the circumstances *might* have forced him to. . . . Of course, the theory didn't cover all the ground, by any means. It didn't explain everything. But it did deal with a number of points in an extraordinarily neat way, which was no doubt why I found it so intriguing.

It also, I realised, answered several of the objections I'd raised when Carol and I had first discussed the frame-up idea in London. I'd argued then that a murderer

couldn't have been sure Fay would follow Arthur out to
the island on the Saturday morning, and that it would
have been quite impossible for him to think up his complicated plan on the spur of the moment when he actually
saw her coming. But now all that was changed. Accepting Carol's assumptions, the blackmailer would almost
certainly have kept an eye on Fay after the photographing incident, to see what happened. He might
well have seen her take the film to the shop on the Friday
—and if so, he'd have guessed she was going to collect it
when she left the house on the Saturday. The likelihood
that she'd follow Arthur out to show him the evidence
would have seemed very great. He could have gone to
the Point and swum to the island with no clear plan of
murder in his mind but with the knowledge that Fay and
Arthur would probably soon be together there. By
chance, Arthur might have been bathing when he arrived
and—assuming he already knew about the diabetes and
the insulin—the sight of the jacket in the sandhills could
have suggested a possible murder method. He could
have taken the insulin and slit the pocket and retired to
the mainland—still not dangerously committed to anything—and there worked out his ingenious frame-up
plan, even to writing the note, on the supposition that
Fay would come. If she hadn't done, he could have
slipped away, and Arthur would eventually have returned
home in the dinghy convinced that he'd lost the insulin by
accident. But she *had*—and by then the blackmailer would
have been all set to move into action. At the first glimpse
of her he could have crossed again to the island, and
hidden there, and waited. He could have watched her
swimming across with the bag held high—with the bag,
I suddenly realised, because the photographs were in it!—

and then pounced on her as she emerged. He could have drowned her by forcing her head under water, faked the dinghy accident, planted the insulin and note in the handbag, abstracted the photograph and negative, and set the boat adrift. Probably the whole thing could have been done in a few minutes. . . . And, assuming the man had noticed that Carol and I were at the house, the telephone call in the evening could have been an impromptu embellishment, an off-the-cuff move that could do no harm and might enormously strengthen the case against Fay if Carol had answered the phone. . . .

Yes, it was a most intriguing theory. For me, though, it had one fundamental weakness. It was built almost entirely on a single discovery—the discovery that the twelfth photograph was missing. If only I'd counted them when I'd first seen them!—if only I'd made a mental note of exactly what photographs had been there! But I hadn't. So now I didn't know whether the twelfth photograph was missing because Carol's hypothetical blackmailer had taken it, or because—in her unswerving determination to convince me of Fay's innocence—she'd taken it herself!

CHAPTER XXII

As soon as lunch was over I left Carol to her coffee and drove into Fairhaven. I didn't doubt her statement that the man in the photograph shop had said he'd charged Fay for twelve prints, but it was something I could check and I checked it. Afterwards I called at the police station and asked if they could tell me where I could get

Inspector Burns on the phone. They gave me a couple of numbers, and I finally tracked him down in a place called Swaffham. He sounded very surprised to hear from me again and when I mentioned the photographs I had the impression that he had to think back quite hard to remember them at all. I asked him just one question—if he'd counted them—and he said he hadn't. It was what I'd expected, for he'd made it clear at the time that he attached no importance to them—and if *I* hadn't thought of counting them, why should he? I thanked him and rang off before he had time to get inquisitive. As far as my nagging suspicion of Carol was concerned, I'd got nowhere.

She was still in the lounge when I returned to the hotel. She didn't ask me where I'd been—a sign, I thought, of our disintegrating relationship. Or else she was too deep in her theory. What she did do was suggest that we should walk out to the Point and have a look at the spot where, according to her, Fay might have done her photographing. I remembered having noticed the broken sea defences Fay had spoken of, but I'd no clear picture of them in my mind so it seemed as good an idea as any. I told the receptionist we'd probably be spending another night at the hotel, and we set off round the wall. In the brisk October wind, the Point looked bleaker than I'd ever known it. The broken defences were almost on the tip. When I came to look at them a second time, I decided they were actually the remains of military defences, probably from the First World War. They didn't amount to much—just a few slabs of concrete sticking up out of the sloping beach a little above high-water mark—but they were enough to set Carol's imagination off again. There was a deep crevice, formed by three concrete lumps, which she said would have been an ideal hiding place for a wad of notes. From above, they would have been invisible. What was more, she said, Arthur *would* have had to kneel down with his back to the creek to push them in—and the blackmailer would have had to kneel to take them out. He might have been photographed in that position—perhaps even with the money in his hand . . . !

I let her run on, and turned my attention to the creek at that spot. Because the beach shelved sharply, it was a place where the water never went out very far, so that anyone waiting in an anchored dinghy probably would have been in a good position to take a photograph. Of course, the higher the tide the nearer it would have been possible to get. . . . I remembered that to-day it had been high water at eleven, and made a rough calculation back to the Thursday before the tragedy. I reckoned it would have been high tide then at about one in the morning—which meant that conditions would have been perfect. Fay would have had no difficulty in getting the dinghy away from the house, and once at the Point she'd have been able to anchor close in. I tried to imagine the scene. Fay waiting in the darkness. . . . Half a minute, though, *had* it been dark? I looked in my diary. Yes—it had been a moonless night—so that was all right. A yard or two out she wouldn't have been visible. But she would have heard a man approaching along the crunchy sand. She would have heard him stop. Judging her moment by sound, she would have let off her flash. Then what . . . ? In that split second, the man would have been both startled and dazzled. He certainly wouldn't have been able to recognise Fay by the light of the flash. But he'd probably have had a torch with him, and after a moment he'd have

turned it on her. He'd have recognised her then all right.
What would he have done? Would he have plunged in
and tried to reach her?   In his clothes, he'd have had
little hope of succeeding—she'd only have had to yank
up the anchor and the boat would have drifted away.
Besides, she'd have had an oar to defend herself with, and
against a man in the water that would have been pretty
effective. The chances were he'd have done nothing.
I could see now why the dinghy would have been such
a good idea—far safer, as Carol had said, than trying to
stalk anyone ashore. It would have made the ideal base.
Indeed, it looked as though from the practical point of
view the whole enterprise could have been both sensible
and feasible. . . . But had it *happened*?
     I very much doubted it.

CHAPTER XXIII

CAROL WAS beginning to feel cold from standing in the
wind, so we crossed to the seaward side of the sandhills
and found a sunny, sheltered spot where she could warm
up before starting back. She had become rather quiet
again, and I guessed she was absorbed once more in the
details of her theory. My own thoughts, as I settled down
beside her, were painfully nostalgic. I couldn't help
recalling the first time we'd visited this spot—that lovely
day in April when we'd picnicked and swum and walked
together in an ecstatic glow of romance and happiness.
How utterly everything had changed! Even Carol's
appearance had changed. Her face had thinned; the
expression of her eyes was harder; her lips were more

compressed. I could scarcely remember when she'd last smiled.

We'd been sitting there for about ten minutes when she suddenly threw off her abstraction. " Well," she said, in a business-like tone, " we've pretty well decided there was a blackmailer. Now we've got to try and *find* him! "

I couldn't take her seriously. I sat gazing out over the brown expanse of the bay. There wasn't a soul about on the Far Sands—there was nothing at all, except a few gulls. Just emptiness. To me, it seemed a symbolic emptiness. That desolate waste, I thought, perfectly matched our chances. . . . But if Carol was bent on a speculative safari, I didn't mind humouring her.

" All right," I said, " let's start. There can't be more than about ten million possibles! "

She looked at me reproachfully. " We won't get far in that frame of mind."

" We won't get far anyway," I said. " What have we got to go on? If Arthur *was* being blackmailed, which I don't believe, we've no idea what his guilty secret was —and we've no way of finding out. We've already put his life under a microscope—we can't do more than that. So there's no lead there. We don't know where the thing happened, if it did happen—or when. We literally haven't a clue."

" I wouldn't go so far as that," Carol said. " There's the point that Arthur's big withdrawals of cash didn't start till a few months ago. . . . That suggests that whatever he was trying to hide may have happened fairly recently."

" It could equally be that the blackmailer had only recently hit on the secret. Or that Arthur had suddenly become more blackmailable because he'd married Fay—

he certainly wouldn't have wanted *her* to know anything unpleasant about him. I still don't see any clue."

She was silent for a moment. Then she said, " Well— perhaps you're right about that. . . . But we do know a few positive things about the man himself."

" Such as? "

" For one thing, he must be a strong swimmer, or he wouldn't have been able to swim to the island."

" True."

" In fact, he must be a powerful man altogether. . . ."

I nodded. A weakling wouldn't have been able to drown Fay and leave so few marks.

" And very active," Carol added. " All those walks he took along the sea wall at night—all that dodging about among the sandhills, and that business with the dinghy. . . . He sounds to me like a fairly young man. Certainly not an old one."

" But experienced and mature," I said. Almost against my will, I was beginning to enter into the spirit of the thing. " Absolutely ruthless, of course. Very resourceful—very cool—a diabolically cunning plotter. Quite an artist, in fact."

" Yes—all that."

" An educated man, too, if we're assuming it was the blackmailer who rang up on the Saturday evening."

" Yes, he had a good accent."

" Definitely no yokel or rough-neck—a polished villain, rather . . . Sophisticated, formidable . . . Hardly a local type, would you say? "

" I shouldn't think so for a moment."

" An urban type? "

" Almost certainly."

There was a little pause. Then I said, " His time would

have had to be his own, of course, with all the coming and
going he'd have had to do. No question of his having to
hold down a job? "

" No, he must have been quite free."

" Probably a man of independent means."

" A successful blackmailer would be, wouldn't he!—
and for all we know he might have had other victims
besides Arthur."

" That's true. . . . Would he have had a wife around,
do you think? I can't quite see him as a family man."

" I shouldn't think a blackmailer would want anyone
around regularly if he could help it," Carol said. " He'd
want privacy to make his arrangements—he'd want to be
able to go off without having to give explanations. . . ."

" A lone operator, in fact. A man who walked alone."

" I should imagine so. . . . You see, James, we *are*
getting somewhere."

" Oh, yes," I said, " we've reduced the possibles to
about a million now! "

She ignored that. " What else do we know about
him? "

" I'd say that's about all."

" Then let's think what *he'd* have to know. That
might help."

I considered for a moment. " Well, as we said before,
he'd have had to know all about Arthur's diabetes."

Carol nodded. " That doesn't narrow the choice much
—anyone who'd spent any time at Embery Staithe would
have been sure to hear about it. Particularly anyone
who was already interested enough in Arthur to blackmail
him. I doubt if he'd even have had to ask questions to
get the information—he could easily have read one of
Arthur's articles, or seen him buying the insulin at the

chemist's, or overheard someone talking about it—Fay, perhaps. . . . Heavens, he might even have talked to Arthur about it himself, if his identity wasn't known . . . ! That's a thought . . . ! Anyway, I don't think it gets us far. What else? "

" Presumably he'd have had to know that Arthur was wealthy," I said, " and that Fay would get the money at his death—otherwise there couldn't have been a convincing frame-up."

" Well, the wealth would have been obvious to every-one, with the fine house and the car and the style of living and so on. . . . And a wife would normally expect to get the bulk of her husband's money, if they'd been on good terms. . . ."

It was innocently said, I told myself—naïvely said. But it shook me. It was like an epitome of all my fears about her.

" So that doesn't get us far either," she said. " Anything else? "

" Your blackmailer would have had to know that Arthur couldn't swim. But he could have seen that for himself with a pair of binoculars—after all, he'd have had to do quite a bit of reconnaissance around here before he could start his blackmailing."

" I suppose so. . . ."

" Oh, yes—he'd have had to choose a suitable hiding place for the money, and satisfy himself there was no danger of other people wandering around there at night, and make himself familiar with the sea wall and sandhills and beaches so that he could use them confidently after dark. He'd certainly never have undertaken a double murder if he hadn't felt he knew the place intimately. . . . I'd say he'd have had to come here quite often."

" And without appearing conspicuous, of course," Carol said. " Perhaps he pretended to be a bird-watcher."

" Perhaps. . . ." I didn't believe for a moment that this macabre game was going to lead anywhere—yet, in an odd sort of way I was beginning to see this man, this imaginary man, quite clearly. A big, muscular, bronzed man of about forty-five, in a well-cut tweed jacket and a cloth cap, taking long, leisurely, observant walks with a pair of glasses, and a haversack over his shoulder! With such protective colouration, he could have counted on passing without much notice. . . .

" Anyway," Carol persisted, " what else would he have had to know . . . ? "

" Well, at the end, of course, he'd have had to know that Fay had taken the film to be developed on the Friday and had gone in again on the Saturday. . . . Possibly that we were in the house on the Saturday night, to make his telephone call worth while. I suppose he *could* have been watching the place from somewhere, though I can't think why. . . ."

" It sounds to me," Carol said, with a frown, " as though he must have been on the watch practically all the time. The house . . . Fay . . . Arthur. . . ." She broke off suddenly. " James, that's another thing—he'd have had to know that Arthur had gone off alone in the dinghy that morning—and Arthur left before eight o'clock ! "

" Yes," I said, " I'm afraid your blackmailer would have had to be an awfully busy chap. Up at all hours ! Out of his fox-hole at crack of dawn ! Always on the spot . . . ! Frankly, Carol, don't you think it's all just moonshine ? "

" No, I don't," she said. Her eyes were suddenly

blazing with excitement. " I think he'd have needed a much better observation post than a fox-hole, that's all. And I think he had one. . . . James, *of course*—he was staying at the hotel! "

CHAPTER XXIV

IF I'D had the slightest belief in the existence of the man, I'd have seized on that suggestion with eagerness—and, indeed, with surprise that we hadn't thought of it before. The hotel, now that Carol had mentioned it, was so obviously the one place from which a blackmailer could have maintained a systematic and absolutely secret watch over the comings and goings, the domestic arrangements and habits, of the Ramsdens. From a bedroom on the east side of the building he could, with good binoculars, have learned as much about what went on in and around the house as though he'd been a guest there—without any risk, and in complete comfort. In the early stages it would have allowed him to choose a moment when Arthur was alone in the house before going out to telephone his threats and instructions. Since there was no night porter at the hotel he could have slipped out quietly at any time to collect the money, with no danger of being seen. On the night when, if Carol was right, he had been photographed, he might well have been able to judge from the way the house lights went out afterwards that there had been no immediate domestic showdown. In the morning he'd have known just when to follow Fay into Fairhaven. From his window, he could have noted Arthur's early departure for the island on the Saturday.

He could have watched Fay drive off again to collect the film, and Maureen go off to catch the Norwich bus, without moving from his bed. Later in the day, after the murder, he could have watched *our* movements, seen the police arrive, decided there was quite a chance that Carol would answer the phone in the presence of the police— and gone out to make his clinching call. From beginning to end, he could have kept his finger comfortably on the pulse of the affair. . . .

All I was doing was considering the theoretical advantages of the hotel—but Carol was already far ahead of me, and planning action. " If he *did* stay at the hotel," she said, " we might be able to discover who he was from the register. . . . Come on, let's go and look." I shrugged, and said, " All right." Working together, however fruitlessly, at least gave me the momentary illusion that we were on the same side. She turned and set off at such a pace that it was all I could do to keep up with her.

The hotel was quiet when we got in. Tea was over, and the cocktail bar hadn't opened yet. Carol suggested that we should check first the numbers of the rooms on the side of the hotel overlooking the house, and we went upstairs. There were four of them—5, 7, 9 and 11. Judging by the short distance between the doors they were all single rooms—which was to be expected, since the double rooms, the best ones, would naturally be on the side with the sea view. We returned to the lobby. There was no sign of the porter, and the reception office was conveniently empty. The hotel register lay on the counter and Carol began to turn back the pages while I stood by in an attitude of studied nonchalance in case anyone should appear. She looked first at the entries around the

murder period. The hotel had still been quite busy in
early October and three of the rooms had been let at
about that time. Number 5 had been occupied by a
T. R. Collins of 318 Cranford Road, Leicester, who had
arrived on the Wednesday. Number 9 had been occupied
by a William Ellis, of Jasmine Cottage, Green Lane,
Treckenham, Suffolk, who had also arrived on the
Wednesday. Number 11 had been occupied by an
F. L. Tandy, of 14a Broad Street, Norwich, who had
arrived on the Thursday. It wasn't possible to tell from
the entries exactly how long any of them had stayed,
since the rooms might have remained empty for a day or
two before the next occupants signed the register—but it
seemed likely from the record that they'd all stayed over
the week-end. None of the signatures bore the least
resemblance to the Italian script of the note found in
Fay's bag, but as the hand had probably been disguised
no conclusion could be drawn from that.

The next thing was to find out if any of the three had
stayed at the hotel before, since our hypothetical blackmailer would presumably have done so—and that took
longer. We had no idea of the dates when the night
walks had taken place, so the only thing was to page back
through the book looking for the same signatures. I
didn't imagine we'd have any success, but in fact we did
find one of them—that of William Ellis. He, it appeared,
had stayed at the hotel many times before. The first
visit had been about nine months earlier, and from the
spring onwards he had been in Norfolk every few weeks.
The fact that he had had Room 9 on each occasion suggested that he was a " regular " and had reserved his
accommodation well in advance. Carol made a note of
the dates.

"Hardly the urban type we had in mind," I said dryly, as she restored the register to its place. "'Jasmine Cottage, Green Lane . . . !'"

"Oh, well, that was only a guess—we could easily have been wrong about it. . . . Besides, how do we know the address is genuine?"

"It doesn't *sound* the sort of address anyone would invent."

Carol had no comment on that. She was already moving on to the next step—a comparison of the dates of Ellis's visits with Arthur's withdrawals of cash. It was an obvious enough idea, though I hadn't thought of it. The village shop was closed, but we got the key of the house from the side door and were soon poring once more over Arthur's bank statement. As we checked the dates a look of deep disappointment crept over Carol's face. The whole period of the withdrawals was roughly the same as the whole period of Ellis's visits, but there was no correlation in the dates. Sometimes the withdrawals had occurred as much as ten days before Ellis's arrival— sometimes just as long afterwards. Carol pointed out, rather desperately, that Arthur wouldn't necessarily have drawn out the money just before each visit—he might even have deliberately avoided doing so, in case Fay should see the bank statement and link the withdrawals with the night walks. He might, as a blind, have withdrawn the money just before the sales were held—and then spent only a part of it. . . . I agreed it was just possible.

There was still one more check we could make—and we both knew it could prove as decisive as our visit to old Mr. Templer had been. We could try to find out what sort of man William Ellis was. I thought the hotel porter would be our best bet, and when he appeared in the lobby just before dinner we got into conversation with him.

" I see you've had a William Ellis staying here," I said, in a casual tone. " I wonder if he could be the William Ellis I met once in Highgate—a little bald man, about sixty, with a cockney accent. . . . Very keen on bird-watching."

" Oh, no," the porter said at once, " Mr. Ellis isn't a bit like that. He's a tall, dark, well-spoken man and he wouldn't be much more than forty. He's interested in grasses."

" Grasses? "

" That's right—he's mad on them. According to him there are more than a hundred and fifty different grasses in this country—you wouldn't think it, would you? He goes around studying them and collecting specimens—all over the place. . . . He thought he'd found a new sort here in the spring—he was as excited as though he'd found a gold mine—but it turned out he hadn't, it was a damaged specimen or something. . . ."

" Fascinating! " I said. " Does he do it for a living? "

" Oh, I don't think so—it's just his hobby. I'd say he's got money—he runs a three-litre Rover and he always does himself very well when he's here."

I gave a false grin. " A bachelor, no doubt! "

" I believe he is, as a matter of fact—he never brings his wife, anyway. . . ."

At that moment the manageress appeared and called " Edward! " and the porter said " Excuse me " and went off.

So there it was. On the evidence we had so far, Ellis

could have been Carol's man—but that was all one could
say. His physical description matched up quite well with
the one we'd worked out for him—but it was hardly
unusual. The fact that he'd stayed at the hotel many
times proved nothing except that he liked the place.
Collecting grasses *could* be a convenient cover for an
itinerant blackmailer—but it was such a recondite hobby
it seemed more likely to be genuine. Certainly we'd
learned nothing that was in any way conclusive.

That, at least, was what I thought. Carol's attitude
was very different. She professed to have hardly any
doubts left. To her, our million suspects had been magi-
cally reduced to one!

CHAPTER XXV

I WASN'T at all surprised when Carol suggested next
morning that we should break our homeward journey at
Treckenham and check up on Jasmine Cottage and its
owner. I felt pretty sure it would be a waste of time, but
as we had to go through Suffolk anyway I could hardly
object.

While I looked up Treckenham on the map and planned
a route, Carol made some more inquiries about Wlliiam
Ellis, which she told me about afterwards. In an attempt
to pin down his movements over the murder week-end she
abandoned subterfuge, tipped the porter lavishly, and
admitted a particular though unexplained interest in
Ellis's activities. Had the porter, she asked, happened to
see him setting off in his car in the direction of Fairhaven
early on the Friday morning? Had he seen him going

off towards the Point on the Saturday morning? Had Ellis been away all that day? But the porter, with the best will in the world, wasn't able to help. Mr. Ellis, he said, reckoned to spend every fine day out of doors, and as it had been fine on the Saturday morning he probably had gone off somewhere. But after a fortnight it was impossible to speak with certainty of any of his move-ments. . . . Even Carol had to accept in the end that the trail at Embery Staithe was cold and that nothing could be got from further questioning there.

We reached Treckenham just before lunch and stopped in the village—it was actually no more than a hamlet—to ask the way to Jasmine Cottage. A schoolboy gave us some rather complicated directions, which I memorised as best I could.

" Do you know who lives there? " I asked. The boy thought for a second. " Yes—Mr. Ellis," he said. I thanked him and he ran off.

I looked at Carol. " Well, there you are—the address is genuine and so's the name. Do you still suspect him? "

" I'd still like to go there," she said.

" I don't see how it can possibly do any good. . . . Look, if Ellis was a blackmailer who was prepared to go to the lengths of a double murder to hide his identity, do you suppose he'd have given his real name and address at the hotel while he was actually on the job? He'd have invented one."

Carol was silent for a moment. Then she said, " He might have thought that was even more dangerous. . . . There'd always be the chance he might run into someone who knew him, and that the false address would be noticed. . . . Anyway, now we're here we might just as well look round."

I shrugged, and drove on.

It took us quite a while to find the cottage. The country through which we were driving was not merely rural—it was incredibly empty. All around us were green, undulating fields, with scarcely a farmhouse visible. The roads were narrow and tortuous and the junctions signposted with names that meant nothing to us. The boy's directions, as I'd feared, proved of little help, and there was no one at all to get fresh ones from. We seemed to be going round and round and getting nowhere. I was just going to suggest we should return to the village and start again when the top of a colour-washed house showed over a hill—the first house we'd seen on the road. At least we could ask our way now. But we didn't have to—the name on the gate was "Jasmine Cottage."

I braked—but Carol said, "Better not stop outside—let's go on a bit and walk back." I thought it a pointless precaution, but I humoured her. There was a wide grass verge a hundred yards farther on and I parked the car there. We walked back slowly, eyeing the cottage. It stood a little above the road, in complete isolation and with a splendid view. It was an extraordinarily pretty place—an old Suffolk cottage of lathe and plaster and ancient timber, with lemon-washed walls, an attractive tapering chimney and a beautifully thatched roof. Beside it was a garage, also thatched. The garden was trim, and bright with autumn flowers. Everything looked perfectly kept. It was a place, evidently, that the owner took great pride in.

We walked on past it, pretending only a casual interest. There was no car in the drive, and from what I could see through the glass windows of the garage there was none there either. Presently we turned and strolled back again. There was no sign of movement, no smoke from the chimney, no sound of life. Carol said, " There's no one there—let's go in and have a look."

We went through the gate and up the neat brick path. It was a very tiny cottage, in a tiny garden, but at close quarters it was even more attractive than it had appeared from the road. The two downstairs rooms were both furnished and decorated in a style to fit the period. Obviously no expense had been spared. One of them was equipped as a study, with hundreds of books and a lot of prints on the walls which at first I couldn't identify but which I realised after a moment were of grasses.

" He's genuine, all right," I said, as we returned to the car.

Carol said, " Let's see if we can find out something about him at the pub in the village."

The saloon bar of the Plough was empty. I ordered our drinks and asked the landlord if he'd care to join us and he said, thanks very much, he'd have a Guinness. We agreed that the weather was extremely good for the time of year. Then Carol said chattily, " We've just been having a look at Jasmine Cottage."

" Oh, yes . . . ? Mr. Ellis's place."

" Is that his name . . . ? An estate agent friend of ours in London heard that it was for sale, so we came down to see."

" For sale . . . ? " The landlord looked doubtful.

" First I've heard of it . . . Mr. Ellis is very attached to the place."

" Oh, dear . . . It could be a mistake, I suppose . . . We couldn't ask him—he wasn't there."

" No, he's away just now. . . . I reckon you'd do better to write."

Carol nodded. " That's what we'll have to do. . . . It's a charming cottage, isn't it? "

" Oh, yes, it's a lovely little place. He's spent a lot of money on it."

" Has he had it long? "

" About three years."

" Do you see much of him? "

" Not a great deal. He's one of those nature chaps— collects grasses, so they say. Always on the move."

" Does he live by himself when he's here? "

" Yes—but he's not usually here for long. It's just his country cottage—he's got another place in London, I believe."

" Has he? " Carol shot me a quick, triumphant glance. " In that case we might be able to get in touch with him by telephone. . . . Do you know whereabouts in London? "

The landlord shook his head. " I don't think I ever heard."

" Who would be likely to know? "

He took a mouthful of Guinness, and pondered. " Well, if anyone knows I reckon it would be the Finneys—Jack Finney does the garden at Jasmine Cottage and his missus cleans the house. They're the only people Mr. Ellis sees much of round here—he's all for peace and quiet."

" Where do the Finneys live? " I asked.

" Why, right across the road. . . ." The landlord pointed through the top pane of the bar window with the stem of his pipe. " See the house with the green door. . . . You'll find Jack at home to-day, too, if you want to talk to him—he's off work with rheumatism."

Carol picked up her bag. " Let's go and see them now," she said. She smiled at the landlord and said, " Good-bye." I finished my drink and followed her out.

We went straight across to the house. A plump, fresh-faced woman answered our knock. We told her our story about having heard that the cottage was for sale and wanting to get in touch with Mr. Ellis and she said we'd better come in and speak to her husband. Mr. Finney was sunk in an easy chair and Carol told him not to get up. He was a long, thin, middle-aged man, slow and stolid and prematurely gnarled with work. He confirmed that Mr. Ellis had a place in London—Mr. Ellis had told him—but he didn't know where it was and he doubted if anyone else in the village knew. If Mr. Ellis wanted to send him any instructions, he said, in reply to Carol, he just sent a postcard. Mr. Finney certainly hadn't heard anything about the cottage being up for sale. The best thing would be to write. Mr. Ellis came down for a day or two every few weeks, so he'd be sure to get the letter. . . . We talked for ten minutes, discovered that both the Finneys thought Ellis was a very nice man, and got a pretty good picture of how he spent his time at the cottage—pottering in the garden, sorting out his grasses, doing a bit of writing, not bothering much about meals, having a good rest. . . . We didn't get anything else.

As we walked back to the car, Carol said, " Well, you

certainly can't say the trip hasn't been worth while. . . .
He *is* an urban type, you see."

" Partly—yes."

" Entirely, I'd say. I'm sure the cottage is only a cover."

" Oh, come! "

" Well, it's just the sort of arrangement a clever black-mailer might make—it would be the perfect first line of defence. It would mean he could always give a genuine name and address, there'd be no danger from returned letters and unanswered inquiries, he could seem to be absolutely on the level—but no one would be able to find him because he'd concealed his real address."

" You can't say he's concealed it," I said. " He merely hasn't told anyone—and if he comes here for quiet week-ends and doesn't see people much I wouldn't expect him to. Not necessarily, anyhow."

" Wouldn't you expect him to put his address on his postcards? "

" People often don't."

" Anyway, if he lives in London why didn't he give his London address at the hotel? Why the cottage, where he spends only a few days occasionally? Isn't that suspicious? "

" I wouldn't say so. We know he travels a lot—he may think of his place in town as just a *pied-à-terre*. He's obviously a countryman at heart, he's proud of the cottage —he probably regards it as his real home. . . . Honestly, I think you're reading far more into this cottage business than it'll stand."

" All right—we'll see," Carol said.

" What do you mean? "

" Well, we can't leave things as they are—we'll have to try and find him, of course."

" That sounds a pretty tall order. . . . Apart from anything else, if your suspicions are right he's probably using a different name in London."

" He may not be. . . . He's got reasonably good cover with the cottage, and it's still true what I said before—if he happened to meet someone he knew under one name, and he was using the other one at the time, he'd be in trouble. I think he may quite easily be William Ellis in London, too."

" If he is," I said, " he won't be the only one! Ellis is a very common name."

" I know—that's probably why he chose it—but we may be able to narrow things down very quickly. If he's the sort of man we think he is—a wealthy, sophisticated blackmailer with luxury tastes—he'd hardly be living in Whitechapel or Notting Hill or Camden Town, would he? He'd almost certainly be in one of the good residential areas—and there can't be so many William Ellises who are."

I looked at her doubtfully. " Well, I'll be most surprised if you get anywhere," I said.

CHAPTER XXVI

I was underrating her, though—her determination, *and* her ingenuity.

The moment we got home she grabbed the telephone directory and turned up the Ellises. There were about twelve columns of them, but by the time she'd sorted out the Williams, and those who by their initials could conceivably have been Williams, there were only two columns. And after an hour's work with a pencil, ticking off those with addresses she regarded as suitable for her mythical blackmailer, she'd reduced the list to a mere thirty names.

" There," she said with satisfaction, " that looks much more manageable."

" What exactly are you planning to do? " I asked her. " Ring them up in turn and ask them if they're blackmailers? "

She frowned down at the list. " I'm not sure that I shall ring them up at all. I don't see how I could find out which one it was without mentioning Embery Staithe or the cottage—and that would put him on his guard...."

" Well, we certainly can't go and wait outside thirty doors till the right sort of man appears! "

" I don't think we'll have to . . . James, where would you say people who live in London mostly park their cars? "

" In the street."

" Exactly . . . ! So if we went along to these thirty addresses at night, and one of them was the right one, we'd probably find a three-litre Rover standing outside. And then we'd know."

It was quite an idea. I said, " Have you any idea what colour his Rover is? "

" Yes, it's a two-tone brown . . . I asked the porter at the hotel."

" H'm . . . Well, it shouldn't be too difficult to check, then. . . ."

" When would be the best time? It wouldn't be much good starting before midnight—he might be out. . . ."

" If we're seen examining people's cars in the early hours of the morning," I said, " we'll probably be run in by the police."

" It needn't be the early hours—we could start at six or seven in the morning, after it's light. We'd be safe enough then—and Ellis would be sure to be in."

" Unless he's on his travels."

" If he's just committed two murders I shouldn't think he'd be collecting any more blackmail money at the moment," Carol said. " He's probably lying low. Anyway, we'll have to take a chance on that . . . James, let's do it to-morrow morning."

I shrugged. If we had to do it, I supposed we might as well get it over. " All right," I said.

We divided the list into two halves so that each of us would have about the same amount of ground to cover. I was to take the northern half. That evening I hired a self-drive car for twenty-four hours and brought it round to the flat. Carol was to use the Lagonda. We arranged with the telephone people to call us at five, and a little after six next morning we were away in opposite directions.

It took me all of two hours to get through my fifteen addresses. One of them was up at Hampstead and one was along the river at Hammersmith and all of them were scattered. Some were in large blocks of flats with parking space in a courtyard in front and I had to be a little discreet in my inspection of the cars. Fortunately there weren't a lot of Rover three-litres—in fact, I only saw two on my round, and neither of them was brown. In an odd sort of way, I found the trip quite exciting. The search for William Ellis had gathered a momentum of its own by now—I wanted to find him, even though I couldn't for the life of me see how finding him would help. But I didn't find him, and I wasn't surprised.

I got back to the flat about nine. The Lagonda, I saw, was already there. Carol was sitting in it, obviously waiting for me. The moment she saw me her face lit up with excitement—and it wasn't questioning excitement. " I found the car," she said. " It's at 104a South Eaton Terrace. Practically round the corner! "

I'd never expected her to pull it off—but now that she had I felt I must see the house for myself, and Carol wanted to see Ellis, if she could do so without showing herself. So after breakfast we took the Lagonda and drove round there. The morning traffic was beginning to build up, but I managed to squeeze the car into a parking space on the opposite side of the road from 104a. Ellis's Rover was still standing at the kerb outside the house. It was a narrow, elegant house on three floors, painted white with a pale yellow front door and with delicate Regency balconies at the upper windows. There was only one bell, which suggested that Ellis occupied the whole of it. We could see no sign of him, so we left the car and crossed the road to take a closer look. A short flight of steps led down to a basement, but there was a Venetian blind over the top part of the window and we couldn't see in. The room at ground level seemed to be a dining-room, and gave an impression of wealth and good taste. We strolled past it once or twice, peering in between the curtains, and then a man suddenly came into the room—presumably Ellis himself—and we retreated. From the car, we continued to watch him for a few moments as he moved around. He was a big, powerfully-built man, with a tanned, good-looking face. Presently he crossed to the window and gazed out and Carol said we'd better go. She was more nervous than ever of being recognised. Anyway, we'd seen all we were likely to see.

As far as I was concerned, the excitement was now over. We'd run our man to earth after an intriguing search and technically that had been quite an achievement—but when I came to take stock of the situation I still couldn't see that finding him had changed anything at all. I went over in my mind every single thing we'd learned about him in the past twenty-four hours and I couldn't think of one that threw the slightest doubt on his genuineness. To me he appeared to be a perfectly open and consistent character. The smart town residence might seem rather far removed from the study of grasses, but there was no reason why a well-to-do bachelor of leisure shouldn't have an outdoor hobby as well as a sophisticated house in Belgravia. The well kept country cottage with its lovely rural setting fitted perfectly into the outdoor picture. Ellis certainly hadn't attempted to hide from anyone that he *had* two places—and he was living under the same name in both. As far as I could see, there was absolutely no reason to imagine he wasn't completely on the level.

Carol, of course, saw the whole thing quite differently. The house was very much the kind of place we'd imagined, she said, when we'd discussed the sort of *milieu* our black-mailer might be living in. It was self-contained, quiet and central. It was bigger than a single man would have needed unless he was conducting some business from there as well. Admittedly it would cost him a fabulous amount to live there—far more than any petty blackmailer could afford—but we'd agreed that our man probably had other sources of income besides Arthur and he could be a very successful practitioner. . . . Carol's tone, as she made her points, was touched with impatience, as though she thought I was being wilfully blind and obstructive. Her view about Ellis seemed to have hardened into conviction since we'd traced him, and she talked as though all we had to do now was find some means of exposing him. Our joint efforts, far from narrowing the gap between us, had actually widened it.

Indeed, the gulf had become so great that it was no longer possible to go on tacitly accepting it as something we could live with. That evening we had the showdown that had been threatening all along.

It was Carol, casting about for some way to clinch her theory, who precipitated it. I was pouring drinks for us both around six when she suddenly said, " James, I'm going to telephone Ellis after all."

" To say what? " I asked in alarm. Visions of a disastrous slander action had leapt at once to my mind.

" Not to say anything—I just want to hear his voice on the phone, to see if it sounds anything like the one we heard at the house. I'll ring off when he speaks."

That sounded harmless enough. " Well," I said, " I doubt if I'd know anyway after all this time—but you go ahead if you think it's worth it. . . ."

I followed her into the sitting-room and she looked up the number and dialled it. She held the receiver a little away from her ear so that I could hear everything. Almost at once a man's voice said, " William Ellis here." It was a clear, confident voice, rather high-pitched, and quite unfamiliar. A couple of seconds passed. Then the voice said, " Hallo—is anyone there . . . ? "

Carol put the receiver down. Her face had clouded.

I said, " It wasn't anything like it. . . . The one thing I do remember about the voice at Embery Staithe is that it was very low."

" He was probably disguising it then," she said. " He'd have been stupid not to—and it's not very difficult, after all, to drop your voice. . . ."

I shrugged. There was no reasoning with her.

" Anyhow," she said, " there must be other ways of checking. . . . Look, suppose I sent him a letter—something that required an answer. I could easily think of an excuse, and I wouldn't need to use my own name. . . . Then we could compare his writing with the note in Fay's bag. There might be some similarity. . . ."

I'd never bothered to tell her what the police had said about that. Now I did. " On the assumption that the Italian script wasn't the man's natural writing," I said, " the view was that there wasn't enough of it to prove anything, even if it could be compared with the real thing. . . . So that wouldn't get you far."

" I see. . . . Well, something else, then. We've got to find something conclusive. . . ."

I lit a cigarette and dropped into a chair. I'd reached *my* conclusion!

Suddenly she said, " James, don't blackmailers often keep something their victims have written? Indiscreet letters—that sort of thing? There might be something like that at Ellis's house. . . . If only we could get in and look! "

" Well, we can't," I said shortly.

" We've got to do something—it's no good simply

saying we can't, now that we've got so far. . . . Perhaps we could get in by some—well—trick. . . . I don't suppose he'd have a housekeeper if he's a blackmailer, but there's bound to be a woman who goes in to clean or something, and he can't be around all the time. . . . We could think up some story to tell her. . . ."

" And ransack his papers . . . ! Carol, it's out of the question—I'll have nothing to do with it. . . . Heavens, do you want to land us both in jail? "

She looked at me hard for a moment. Then she said, " All right—then I'll tell the whole story to the police and get *them* to search. If I tell them all we know . . ."

" We don't know anything," I said.

" But of course we do. . . ."

" Not a thing. If you went to the police they'd laugh at you—or just be sorry for you. . . . From their point of view, Fay's guilt is established. As far as she's concerned, the case is closed. They'd pay no attention to your wild accusations—and they certainly wouldn't take any action. How could they? "

" But all the evidence . . ."

" There isn't any evidence—not a shred. . . . You might as well face it, Carol—it's the truth. All there is is a fantasy you've dreamed up. . . . Oh, I know it's followed a sort of logical pattern in a way, and there've been one or two rather odd discoveries—and I've gone along with you in the hope that something more solid might turn up. But it hasn't."

" What about the missing photograph . . . ? That's evidence, isn't it? "

" Who can prove it was missing? " I said. " If you went to the police with a theory based on the loss of the photograph—a theory obviously designed to clear Fay's name—they'd be certain to think you'd taken it your-self."

She stared at me. "But that's fantastic. *You* know I didn't . . ." She broke off. "*Don't* you?"

I hesitated—and that was enough. She said, "Oh, my God!" and turned away.

I said, "I'm sorry, Carol, but it's no use pretending the thought hadn't occurred to me. You'd so obviously have done anything to convince me. . . ."

There was a little silence. Then she said, in a flat voice, "So you've absolutely no belief in my theory—or in me?"

"I'm afraid I've no belief in your theory. . . . Carol, I'd give my life to prove you right, but I can't go on kidding myself. . . . You've produced an alternative that *might* have happened—but that's all. You've done it by a sort of logical sleight of hand—twisting things in your favour all the time. *Making* them fit. Working back-wards from the conclusion you wanted to reach. It's not good enough. Your theory's ingenious—almost too ingenious—but it's empty. It's got no substance to it— it's just a string of assumptions. All the solid evidence still points to Fay having killed Arthur—and I think she did!"

"And you think I'm like her," Carol said slowly. "A rapacious little schemer who's got her claws into you for your money and won't let go!"

"I never said that. . . ."

"But it's what you think. I know it is—I suppose I've known it all the time. . . . It's been in your face—all through these ghastly days. You think I've done all this just to convince *you*. . . . Well, at least we've got the position straight now. Obviously I can't expect any more help from you." She turned abruptly, and went into the bedroom, and closed the door.

I didn't attempt to follow her. I'd absolutely nothing to say.

When, just before eight, I called out to ask her if she intended to come out to dinner, she said she wasn't hungry and told me to go on my own. I drove to a little restaurant I'd sometimes used in my bachelor days and had a grim and solitary meal. Afterwards I walked round the block a few times. I couldn't see even a chink of light in the situation now. Carol and I had finally reached a dead end.

I got back to the flat about nine-thirty. There was a note on the hall table. It said:

" James, I'm leaving you. I'm sure you'll agree it's the only thing to do. Without trust, our being together is just a mockery. I love you, and I think I always shall—but I can't see any future in it. For now, at any rate, good-bye. C."

CHAPTER XXVII

So CAROL had decided we'd reached a dead end, too! I felt pretty shattered—and illogically surprised. Or *was* it so illogical? True, an eventual split-up had seemed more than a possibility ever since Arthur's murder—but I hadn't supposed that Carol would make the first move. That didn't make sense. If she was prepared to walk out before she had to, for the sake of her dignity and pride—to

abandon everything at a stroke without a thought for her
material interests—what became of my idea that her sole
purpose in defending Fay so vigorously had been to
convince me, to win me over, so that she could stay?
The two things simply didn't square.

For a moment, I almost believed in her again. Then
I re-read the note. It was crisp and decisive—but there
was nothing final about it. . . . " For now, at any rate,
good-bye." It could hardly have been less final. I had
a quick look round the flat to see what she'd taken with
her. All she'd done was throw a few things into a case.
She might well come back, in her own time. It could be
a try-on—a bluff—just to show me how much I'd miss
her. . . . And I *would* miss her, there was no doubt of
that. . . . A softening-up move . . . ? But if that was her
idea, wouldn't she have tried the more usual methods
first—tears, protestations, appeals? Or did she think the
abrupt departure, the sharp absence, would prepare me
more effectively for the next assault? If so, she might
well be right. . . . I was back where I had been, on a
mental see-saw, lonely and wretched and corroded
with doubt.

Perhaps this was the moment when *I* should make a
move? Perhaps it would be better if I gave her no chance
to return and start the arid argument all over again?
This, surely, was the moment to accept the break-up, to
go right ahead, see a lawyer, make the separation final.
It would be spineless, I told myself, to dither any more.
I had my life to live, my interrupted career to think of.
I must pull myself together. I must make myself face up
to the fact that my marriage was finished.

But I couldn't face up to it—not yet, anyway. Instead,
through the blank evening, I found myself going over all

the old ground again. The case against Fay, so complete, so detailed, so convincing. The case that Carol had fabricated against Ellis, so utterly speculative. What *did* it in fact amount to? That he'd been in the right place at about the right time, that he'd known the district, that he'd been in a position to watch the Ramsdens if he'd wanted to, that he matched up physically to an imaginary picture we'd drawn of a purely hypothetical blackmailer. That was all. As an indictment, it was pathetic.

I tried once more to imagine a blackmailer resorting to a particularly hazardous double murder, knowing the fearful penalty that would follow discovery, simply to avoid a sentence of a few years—and I could only see it as stupendous folly. Not even a sentence—the *risk* of a sentence. And a small risk, I thought again, if it arose solely from the fact that his identity was about to become known to his victim. A blackmailer's safety, as I'd said to Carol, depended on the *hold* he had, the fear he could impart. Many blackmailers were known to their victims, and it never seemed to worry them unduly. In Arthur's case, the hold of a blackmailer wouldn't have been appreciably weakened even if Fay had managed to take his photograph. Fay would no doubt have extracted Arthur's secret on the strength of it, and she might well have had her own views on what they ought to do—but she'd have been loyal. She certainly wouldn't have rushed off to the police. . . .

It was then that I was struck by an entirely new thought. Suppose the secret had been essentially a secret *from* Fay. Suppose, for instance, that Arthur had been involved in his youth in some particularly sordid episode with a woman. Suppose his behaviour had been not

L

criminal but utterly squalid and contemptible—the kind
of thing he could look back on only with shame and
humiliation. If so, I could well believe he'd have given
anything for Fay not to know. Her love and admiration
had meant so much to him that it was quite on the cards
he'd have paid blackmail money to keep the secret from
her when he wouldn't have done so to keep it from
anyone else.

In that case, of course, the situation would have been
very different. Once Fay, using the photograph as a
lever, had got the truth from Arthur, the blackmailer's
hold *would* have gone—and he'd have known it. Arthur
would at once have become a kind of lapsed client, with
nothing to lose—and he'd have been as dangerous as a
grenade with the pin out. So the blackmailer would
have had to prevent Fay reaching Arthur with the
photograph—and the only way would have been to kill
her. But with Fay dead, Arthur would again have had
nothing to lose—so he'd have had to be silenced, too.
Only a double murder, in fact, would have ensured that
the blackmailer would keep his freedom.

It was an exciting idea. It was certainly a vast im-
provement on Carol's theory, which to my mind had
never adequately accounted for Arthur's murder. It even
tied up well with the fact that the first of Arthur's big
cash withdrawals had occurred only after his marriage
to Fay. . . . But was it true? Wasn't I just weaving airy
patterns, as Carol had done?

My thoughts turned again to Carol, to her behaviour.
To her vehement, undeviating faith in Fay from the
start. Her attitude had *seemed* genuine—but so had Fay's
to Arthur. A good act could seem more sincere than
sincerity. About one thing I felt more sure than ever—

she *knew* the truth about Fay. It was there in her heart. If only there were some way of drawing it out, of testing her. . . .

In a sense, I realised, she had been tested. She'd suggested going to extreme limits to prove her theory. She'd suggested going to the police. *Why?* If she knew her theory was false, would she have wanted to push it that far? Would she have wanted the police to search Ellis's house and find it barren of evidence? How would that have helped her with me? Wouldn't she have done better to stop at the theory itself . . . ? But then, of course, she'd probably have realised as well as I did that the police would take no action. Her bold suggestion could easily have been one more bit of bluff.

I thought again about the photographs. That missing picture could have been the one really solid and arresting fact, if I'd had no doubts about Carol. *If!* How could I be sure . . . ?

My mind went back to the events of that afternoon at Embery Staithe . . . Carol's flushed excitement, so easy to assume . . . her skilful lead-in to the fact that the photograph was missing . . . her well-thought-out conclusions. . . . She'd been as smooth and competent as a good conjurer, sure that she was safe from detection. . . .

Suddenly, I paused. *Had* she been so safe? Suppose, when I'd rung up Burns and asked him if he'd counted the photographs, he'd said he had! Suppose he'd said that all twelve had been there. Then I'd have *known* that Carol had taken the missing one herself. . . . If she'd been going to take it, wouldn't she first have rung Burns herself and made sure he didn't know how many there'd been? It wouldn't have been difficult for her. . . . But she certainly hadn't done, or he'd have mentioned it.

She might have taken a chance, of course. She'd have known it was very unlikely he'd have bothered to count them. But would she have risked it? Perhaps she'd simply overlooked the point. If so, it was about the only thing her subtle mind had overlooked.

I was more troubled than ever now. Momentarily, the balance seemed to have tipped in Carol's favour. Had I, after all, got my deadly syllogism wrong? Should it have been, " Carol is genuine. Fay was exactly like Carol. Therefore Fay was genuine " ?

I thought again of Ellis. One thing was clear—he was the only alternative suspect in the picture. It was Ellis, or no one. If he could once be eliminated, all doubts would be set at rest. Then it would have to be Fay. Then I could stop torturing myself. . . . If only, I thought, there were some way of putting *him* to the test —some simple, practical, discreet way of checking on him, of proving his guilt or innocence . . . ! There ought to be. A guilty man would surely be vulnerable in many ways. . . .

Vulnerable! . . . As I said the word over to myself, a perfectly fantastic idea came into my mind.

Suppose *I* tried to blackmail *him*!

CHAPTER XXVIII

AT FIRST I regarded it as one of those crazy ideas that rush into the mind sometimes only to be instantly dismissed. I couldn't begin to imagine myself doing it. I hadn't any of Carol's histrionic talent—I'd never be able to carry it off. I'd make an utter mess of it. I might easily get into the most frightful trouble. In any case, I wouldn't be justified. Demanding money with menaces —even experimentally—was a revolting thing to contemplate. Any man, however innocent, might feel disturbed and upset at having it done to him. I simply hadn't the right.

Then I wondered. If someone were to try to blackmail me about a murder I knew nothing of, I wouldn't be very disturbed, I decided. I'd think the man was a lunatic, or that he'd mistaken me for someone else. I'd probably tell the police, and then put the thing out of my mind. Ellis would no doubt do the same. He hadn't looked to me like a man who'd be easily upset.

And, of course, if by some unthinkable chance he was guilty, he deserved no consideration anyway.

I continued to turn the idea over. After all, I told myself, why shouldn't I be able to do it? It would all be by telephone—and putting over an act would be much simpler on the phone than face to face. I'd only have to say a short piece and ring off. Accuse him, pretend I wanted money, and instruct him where to take it—that was all. It probably wouldn't be anything like as dangerous as I'd thought—certainly not as dangerous as trying to get past Ellis's cleaning woman and rifling his papers. I might have to disguise my voice a bit—for all I knew he might have been at the Fairhaven inquest and heard it—but I could practise that. He wouldn't have a clue who I was. And if I rang him from a public call-box, there'd be no chance of his tracing me.

It would be an ordeal, undoubtedly—an ordeal I shrank from with almost physical revulsion. It would be all the harder because I had no firm belief in Ellis's guilt to sustain me. But the alternative was to do nothing— and *never to know*.

That was the thing. Always, as long as I lived, there'd be the spark of doubt—the dreadful feeling that I might —just *might*—have wrecked two lives through a cowardly failure to do what was open to me. That way, I'd never know peace of mind again.

I mulled over it most of the night. By next day, I'd got to the stage of mentally selecting a telephone box, and a suitable time, and of planning what I might say. The timing was easy—I would feel safer doing it after dark, and around nine in the evening would be a quiet period in the streets. If Ellis wasn't at home the first time I could always ring him again later. What to say was another matter. I'd have to disclose enough to convince him I knew everything—supposing there was anything to know—but I'd have to keep my facts as broad as possible to avoid small errors that might expose me as a mere guesser. I spent hours preparing and rehearsing a trenchant little speech, and how I'd put it over—if ever I reached that point. I still hadn't made up my mind, and I had some bad moments of panic during the day when I almost decided to call the whole thing off. But in the end my urge to settle the affair one way or the other was stronger than my fears. The bleak emptiness of the flat helped to drive me on. As nine o'clock came round, I knew I'd got to try.

There was a quietish square a block or two away from the flat, with a railed garden in the centre and a phone kiosk half-way along one side. It took me only a couple of minutes to reach the square and I went straight to the box. It was unoccupied, and there was no one about. I slipped inside, feeling already like an apprehended criminal, and dialled Ellis's number. As his phone began to ring I almost hoped he wouldn't be at home—but he was.

" William Ellis here," he said.

I spread a handkerchief over the mouthpiece of the phone, pressed button A, and dropped my voice to an artificially low key which I hoped would sound sinister. " Ah!—Mr. Ellis," I said. " You don't know me, but I know you. I'd have rung you up before, but it's taken a little time to trace you . . ."

" Who are you? "

" I'm afraid I can't tell you that . . ."

" What do you want? " His tone was sharp, now—as, indeed, mine would have been in his place!

" I want some money," I said, " and I mean to have it. I happened to be watching from the sandhills when you killed Fay Ramsden the other day."

There was a moment of absolute silence. I waited tensely. There were several ways an innocent man might respond. With incredulity, anger, curiosity. . . .

Ellis said, " Well, let's discuss it, by all means . . . Hold on a moment, will you? "

I heard the receiver being laid down at his end—and

then a faint sound like a door being opened or shut. Sweat started to roll down my face. He was probably getting someone to call the police on another line—his tone had been altogether too mild. I'd wanted to hear his reaction, but I wished now I'd made my speech right away. It might be only a matter of a minute or two before the call was traced and a squad car arrived outside the box. I'd have a hell of a time explaining! I'd do better to hang up, and run for it. . . . But perhaps he was only shutting the door. Perhaps he was standing there now by his phone, trying to think what to say and do. I glanced apprehensively out into the street. A man and a girl were walking by on the other side, but otherwise the square seemed empty. I'd give him another thirty seconds. I transferred the slippery receiver to my right hand, and looked at my watch. Thirty seconds—not a moment longer . . . !

Suddenly Ellis said, " Hallo . . . Are you still there? "

I had to say my piece quickly now, and I poured it out. " Listen," I said, " I've been keeping an eye on you in Norfolk for a long while. I know you were blackmailing Arthur Ramsden and I know why. I know you've been picking up money from him every few weeks for some time. I know Fay Ramsden took your photograph. I saw you swim across to the island that Saturday. I saw you drown Fay Ramsden and put the insulin in her bag and fix the dinghy to look like an accident . . . Well, now it's my turn. I want five hundred pounds to keep quiet, and these are your instructions. To-morrow night, at exactly eleven o'clock, you'll leave the money where you used to collect it from Ramsden. If you don't show up, the police will have the whole story by next morning. And it'll be your funeral—literally. A double murder can be a hanging matter, don't forget . . . One last word —don't try any tricks. *I* know the ropes, too . . . Good night, Mr. Ellis."

I rang off before he had a chance to say anything, and slipped out of the box. A car was just coming round the end of the square, at speed. I couldn't see whether it was a police car or not, but I hadn't much doubt. I knew I hadn't time to walk away. I dived behind the box and scrambled over the fence into the dark garden. I ran across it and climbed back into the square on the other side. The car had stopped and I could hear men's voices—but no one had spotted me. With my heart slamming like a pile driver, I walked as quickly as I could back to the flat.

CHAPTER XXIX

I POURED myself a stiff shot of whisky and gulped it neat. It had been a near thing and I still felt shaken. Now that it was over I could scarcely believe I'd done it. I must have been off my head! Especially to carry on after Ellis had said he'd like to discuss it! *Of course* he wasn't a blackmailer. He'd behaved as any good citizen would have done—playing for time—getting the telephone pest to hang on while he took steps. . . . I'd been damned lucky—it was a miracle I wasn't in a cell. . . . I lit a cigarette and inhaled deeply. Well, there was one thing about it—at least I wouldn't have to follow it up now. There was obviously no point in my going to Norfolk as I'd planned. I could forget the whole thing. . . .

Then uncertainty returned. Wouldn't a guilty Ellis

have wanted to discuss the matter at least as much as an innocent one?—and couldn't there have been all sorts of reasons for the delay? He might have had a guest in the house—he might have gone to make sure the conversation wouldn't be overheard—he might even have gone to another room, to a phone extension, where he could talk privately. I wouldn't have known. . . . And I couldn't be *sure* that the car had been a police car. It could just as well have been a couple of men driving up to one of the houses. I ought to have waited in the garden and made certain, because if it had been a police car that would have put Ellis in the clear for good. . . . But I'd panicked, and lost my chance of that—and I still hadn't *proved* anything. Basically, nothing had changed. If it had been worth ringing Ellis in the first place, wasn't it still worth going through with it?

I didn't know. Fortunately I didn't have to decide that night. I'd make up my mind to-morrow.

There was no word from Carol in the morning. If I'd known where to find her I'd have told her what I'd done. Oddly, I missed being able to consult her. As it was, I'd have to decide alone. When I got down to it, it wasn't difficult. My mind was fresh after a fair night's sleep, and I saw the position more sharply than I had the night before. It still seemed to me overwhelmingly probable that Ellis was innocent—but it was more clear than ever that I hadn't proved anything. The doubt was still there. All I'd done was create the conditions for proving something, as I'd intended. If Carol's theory was right—if Ellis was a blackmailer and a murderer and my thumbnail account of his actions had been near the truth—it was almost certain that he'd go to Norfolk.

I'd shown such knowledge that he wouldn't dare not to.
With less at stake, he might have gambled on his telephone
caller not wanting to go to the police with an eye-witness
story two weeks late—but not when his life was in jeopardy.
If he was guilty of a double murder, there was no question
about it—he'd *have* to go. . . . And if he didn't show up,
that would be the end of the theory. Whatever happened, the test would work. Once and for all, I'd *know*.
I'd made the opportunity—and if I failed now to follow
it up, I'd always regret it.

Once I'd reached the decision, I quickly made my
plans. I'd drive up right away, I decided, and pick a
secure base in the sandhills while it was still daylight and
I could see what was happening around me. Slight
though the prospect was, I'd no desire to risk bumping
into a desperate murderer in the dark. It would mean
a long vigil in raw weather, so I dressed warmly and put
a heavy overcoat in the car. I made some sandwiches
and a flask of coffee and stuffed them into a rucksack,
together with my binoculars and the biggest torch I could
find. I'd want something to read, and I chose a volume
from the shelves and stuck it in with the food. By ten
o'clock I was ready. I'd drive to Fairhaven, I decided,
and leave the car there, and approach the Point from that
side. I didn't want to be seen at Embery Staithe, where
I might easily meet someone I knew and have to think
up an explanation of why I was there.

I reached Fairhaven just before two and parked the
Lagonda on the quay with a lot of other cars. Naturally
there was no sign of Ellis's Rover. A boisterous wind
had got up and there were white horses in the channel
that led to the harbour. The prospect was about as un-

THE FAR SANDS**

inviting as it could be—and my chances as unpromising.
I reckoned the odds against Ellis turning up at the Point
that night were so big they'd have to be calculated in
light-years.   For a moment I was tempted to abandon
the whole crazy enterprise.   But I'd come a long way—
and it was still true that nothing had changed funda-
mentally.   I'd have to see it through.   I managed to get
a good lunch at a pub, which fortified me, and soon after
three I collected the rucksack from the car, and a thick
stick for companionship, and set off along the shore of
the bay in the direction of the Point.   The tide was well
up, and I had to keep close to the sandhills.   It was about
four miles round the bay, a plodding march.   From time
to time I climbed to a height and swept the ground ahead
and behind me with my glasses.   There wasn't a soul
about anywhere.

I reached the Point just before five and established
myself in a hollow near the top of the highest sandhill,
close to the look-out that I'd climbed to with Arthur.
Below me, twenty yards away on the landward side of the
dunes, were the broken slabs of concrete.   It was as good
a position as I could hope to find.   The tossing sea looked
grey and cold but I had shelter from the wind and at least
there was no rain.   I made myself as comfortable as
I could, with my overcoat drawn closely around me, and
settled down to wait.   Until the light faded, I read the
book I'd brought.   There was a lot in it about causeless
melancholy.   I wished mine had been causeless.

When it got dark I had some food and coffee and cau-
tiously smoked a cigarette.   The sky had begun to clear
with the dusk and a few stars were coming out.   There'd
be no moon, I knew, but at least the night wouldn't be
pitch black.   I sat listening to the wind and the moan of

the now distant sea, and watching the lights of Fairhaven across the Far Sands, and wondering where Carol was and what she was doing. . . .

It was a cold, interminable wait, with nothing pleasant to occupy my thoughts, nothing to raise my spirits. I could have borne it with fortitude if there'd been anything good to look forward to at the end of it—but I knew there wasn't. The only outcome I could sensibly hope for was the dismal satisfaction of negative proof. . . . Yet, as the hours crept by and ten o'clock came and went, I became aware of a faint, apprehensive chill that had nothing to do with the temperature. The place was so incredibly lonely. The mere thought that someone else might be lurking in the sandhills, listening, watching, waiting, was enough to send icy tremors down my spine.

As eleven o'clock drew near, the strain became almost unbearable. I began to hear imaginary sounds—the crunch of stones, I thought at one moment, beside the creek. I peered through my glasses into the darkness. They weren't much good at night but they were better than nothing. I could see the edge of the water beyond the broken concrete. I could just make out the shape of the blocks. For a moment I thought I could see a darker shape on the ground, and I reached nervously for my stick—but it didn't move, it was only flotsam. Of course there was no one there. I was jittery, that was all.

I looked at my watch again, shining the torch on it for a second under my coat. Ten minutes past eleven! Of course he wasn't coming. If he'd ever intended to, he'd certainly have been punctual. I listened. The only sounds were of the sea and the wind and the gently-stirring marram grass. I was just a damned fool, I told myself, to be sitting out here in the cold on a late October night—for nothing. I'd give him ten minutes more, and then get back to the car. . . .

At that moment, a voice shattered the silence. It wan't an ordinary voice—it was raucously distorted, terrifyingly loud. It was coming through a loud hailer! It said, " Listen, whoever you are! This is a police officer. We've got you surrounded. Better come out quietly and give yourself up."

For a second, I lay in paralysed immobility. So this was the pay-off! Ellis was innocent, as I'd always supposed—Fay was guilty. He'd told the police about the rendezvous, and they'd come to get me. I ought to have thought of it. . . Now it was too late. . . .

Or was it? I might still have a chance. They didn't know who I was. If once I could give them the slip I'd be all right. It was worth trying. The sandhills were a maze of tracks through the grass. . . . I began to gather up my things—any of them could be used to trace me if I left them. It was difficult to pack them quietly in the darkness. The binoculars clinked against something. . . . I waited, scarcely daring to breathe. All right . . . I was ready now. I began to inch my body forward through the cold, soft sand, pushing the rucksack and stick ahead of me. My passage wasn't noiseless, but it was the best I could do. . . .

Suddenly the loud hailer crackled again. " I can hear him, Inspector—he's moving your way, I think." The voice was coming from a different direction this time. I stopped. Silence fell. They were all listening. " Better come out, blackmailer," the voice said. " We're closing in on you—you haven't a chance. You'll only make things worse for yourself. Come out!—walk out on to the beach and show a light."

If the night had been really dark I'd have got up and made a dash for it, but it wasn't, and with the police all around I knew I hadn't a hope. I switched my torch on and slithered down on the seaward side of the bank and walked out on to the open beach. A moment later another torch flicked on and a figure loomed up, crunching towards me with heavy tread.

I started to walk towards him. He seemed to be alone. Suddenly I stopped still. *Fool!* If Ellis was ignorant of the whole business, how would he have known that *this* precise spot would be the place to send the police to. *This* spot, so close to where Arthur had hidden the money. He *couldn't* have known.

I'd almost left it too late. The dark figure was rushing at me. His right hand was raised—he had some weapon. I dived for his legs. The blow that was aimed at my head landed on my left shoulder with terrific force, completely numbing my arm. But my right hand had found his ankle and I jerked him to the ground. For a moment or two we struggled like animals in the sand. He kept striking at me with the metal thing he was holding, but he was too close to do much damage. I landed one solid jab on his face, but that was all. Crippled, I hadn't a chance. I tore away from him, and he came at me with his weapon raised again. I ducked and weaved and went staggering away across the sand. . . . Suddenly I knew I ought not to be trying to fight him. I'd nothing to gain. I knew all I needed to know. It was *he* who'd got to make it a fight to a finish. With two murders behind him, he'd got to kill me. I swung away and raced off down the beach, across the sand, towards the lights of Fairhaven. My legs, at least, were whole.

CHAPTER XXX

FOR A few moments I pounded along with Ellis only a
yard or two behind me. I was badly hampered by my
overcoat but I dared not slow down to get rid of it—if
I paused for an instant he'd be on me. At least he was
wearing a coat too, so he had the same handicap. A
little feeling was beginning to creep back into my left
arm. I could move it. Things might have been worse.
But I'd no room to manœuvre, no room to try and double
back, no alternative but to keep going straight ahead
across the sand-whipped beach and hope I wouldn't
stumble in a hole or soft patch. That would finish
everything.

In fact, it was Ellis who stumbled first. I heard him
give a grunt as he pitched forward. He was up almost
at once, but in that couple of seconds I had time to shed
my coat. It was worth the yard or two I'd have gained
by keeping going. I put on a spurt, and from the sound
of his feet I could tell that a gap had opened between us.
If I could widen it a bit more I'd be able to work round
to the safety of the sandhills. But not yet. I kept going.
I was having to fight now for every breath. I could hear
Ellis panting, too. It was a deadly pace, and the going
was getting heavier every second. We'd left the firm
beach and were ploughing through banks of soft, deep
sand that dragged at the ankles. Between the banks were
shallow channels, with a tugging flow of tide. The Far
Sands, I thought, and a flowing tide! And far worse

ground ahead—deeper channels, with precipitous sides, just the place for breaking a leg! I must get out of this. I veered a little to the right, but not much, because every time I left the straight line it gave Ellis the inside track and he gained on me.

I staggered on, trying not to think how tired I was, trying to concentrate on the contours of the ground and nothing else. We must be a long way from the dunes now. The noise of the sea was much louder and the wind was howling like a banshee across the open flats. The sand was beginning to have a sodden feeling. Abruptly, before I could check my headlong pace, emptiness yawned in front of me and I plunged forward. The next moment I'd hit water, deep water, and was having to swim. This must be one of the channels that ran into Fairhaven. I heard Ellis crash into the water behind me. There was a sluicing current and I swam with it, but a little across. My left arm was still pretty useless and my clothes were a fearful drag—but Ellis's overcoat would be worse. He couldn't possibly last long. . . . Then there was sand underfoot again and I was out and struggling forward once more. Ellis had made it, too—he was coming on. He couldn't do anything else. He'd never give up.

I had little idea where we were now. Somewhere out in the vast waste, that was all I knew—with the tide racing in, cutting the sand into islands with swirling deeps between. Lost in the Far Sands, in near darkness! I swerved away to the right. Suddenly I pitched forward again—and once more I was struggling in icy water, out of my depth. The tide was fiercer here than ever. I hadn't the breath to swim—I had to let myself float with it. My sodden clothes began to drag me down. I no

M

longer thought of the human enemy. I didn't even
know what had happened to him. It didn't matter any
more. This was going to be the end for both of us. . . .
Then I felt something hit me—something solid in the
water. Incredibly, it seemed to be stationary. The
water was rushing past it. It was one of the buoys that
marked the main channel. I clung to it, desperately.
Then something long and dark, like a spar, came sweeping
down on me out of the roaring night. It bumped against
me, and I saw that it was Ellis—face downwards, motionless, with the overcoat round him like a shroud. For a
moment the body stayed with me, held against the
buoy. Then it swung round in the stream, and disappeared.

I clung to the buoy for a few seconds, getting my breath
back. The short respite gave me new strength, new hope.
With Ellis no longer blocking the line of retreat, there was
still a chance. If I kept the distant lights of Fairhaven at
my back, I might be able to retrace my steps before the
sea caught up with me. But first I had to reach solid
ground. I let go of the buoy and struck out in the direction where I thought the bank should be. The tide still
gripped me, but I couldn't be far from the shallows.
I put all I had into a few last strokes. I was almost spent
when I touched bottom and struggled out into a mere
foot of water. The surface was broken, and short,
curling waves slapped at me with vicious force. I stripped
off my jacket and trousers and checked my bearings with
the lights and plunged on. The tossing sea was all
around me now. It was a dreadful place. I quickly lost
all sense of distance and of time. Somewhere, I knew,
there was that first channel ahead of me—wider and
deeper than it had been. For me, it was the Jordan—if

I could once get back across it I'd be safe. I'd *got* to make it. I'd too much to live for to fail. I struggled on, shuffling and stumbling through the shallow sea. . . . Suddenly I was falling again. My head went under. I gathered up my last reserves of strength and fought my way forward. The bank was shelving—I could feel the bottom. I scrambled out and ploughed on through the waves. The water grew shallower. Now it was only ankle deep. I was out, and on to the beach. I'd done it!

For a few moments I lay in the lee of the sandhills, too exhausted to move. But with no clothes except a singlet and briefs, and those wet, I knew I *had* to move. Where to? Not Fairhaven—I was too spent to walk round the bay. The house on the creek!—that would give me shelter for the night. I staggered up and set off round the sea wall, swaying and blundering like a drunken man. When I reached the house I broke a window and climbed in. The electricity was cut off but I groped around and found some matches, and then some brandy. I swallowed a couple of mouthfuls, and went upstairs, and wrapped myself in a cocoon of blankets, and sank at once into a stupor of sleep.

CHAPTER XXXI

IN THE MORNING, I looked and felt a physical wreck. My face was puffed up from the blows I'd got in the fight, my eyes were bloodshot from the wind and salt, my lips were raw. There was a huge purple weal across my shoulder where Ellis's murder weapon had landed, and

I was so stiff that at first I could hardly move. But my
spirits were soaring. Wonderfully, unbelievably, the
nightmare had passed. There was bound to be some
difficult explaining to do, and perhaps a grim time ahead
for a bit—but that didn't matter. All I could think of
was that the gulf between Carol and myself was closed.
Miraculously, she'd been right—and in the end, it was
I who'd proved her right. I could scarcely wait to
find her.

I bathed my face, and shaved delicately with Arthur's
things, and found an old jacket and trousers in a cupboard
that were a tight fit but wearable, and when I'd made
myself reasonably presentable I caught a bus into Fairhaven and went straight along to the police station. I
said I had two murders and an accidental death to report
and gave the sergeant a sufficiently circumstantial
account of what had happened to bring Inspector Burns
rushing over from Norwich within the hour. He took
me into a private office where we wouldn't be disturbed
and I started my story at the beginning and went right
through to the end.

At first he seemed quite unable to believe it. He looked
at me as though he thought I'd taken leave of my senses,
his shrewd eyes contantly wandering over me before
returning to mine in dubious appraisal. But whatever
he thought of my sanity he had to investigate, and soon
the wheels began to turn. In next to no time a search
party had left to see what it could find along the beach,
and a police car had been dispatched to look for Ellis's
Rover. While they were away a doctor examined me and
treated my shoulder and afterwards I was given a much-
needed meal, so that I felt ready for the next round.

The searchers returned in the late morning with Ellis's

body, which had been washed up quite near to Fairhaven. They also brought in most of the impedimenta we'd discarded on the beach and across the sands—my rucksack and stick and sodden clothes, the two torches, the portable loud hailer that Ellis had taken with him to the Point to flush me out, and a spanner they'd picked up on the edge of the main channel. It looked harmless enough as it lay on the table, but it would have cracked my skull for a certainty if Ellis had landed that first savage blow on my unsuspecting head, as he'd intended. Only my last-minute doubt about him had saved me.

Now that Burns had a body on his hands, he'd become very uncommunicative. I knew he'd had a long talk with Scotland Yard during the morning, but he wouldn't tell me what had been said. He seemed pretty suspicious of me, and though I told him I was anxious to get back to London as soon as possible in case Carol returned home, he showed no sign of being prepared to let me go. I had to make a full statement, which was taken down and typed and read over to me before I signed it, just as though it had been a confession. They were behaving almost as though *I'd* been responsible for Ellis's death. They even asked me if I'd ever owned a loud hailer! The atmosphere improved a little when they found Ellis's car parked beside a creek near Fairhaven and discovered from a gap in the tool kit that the spanner was definitely his —but they were still wary.

Then, around five, Burns brought another man into the room where I'd been reading and waiting. He introduced the newcomer as Superintendent Dobson, of the Yard. The superintendent was a towering, massively formidable man approaching sixty. He was grim, but not unfriendly, and as we sat down he offered me a cigarette. Burns lit it for me. Things were looking up!

"Well, Mr. Renison," Dobson said, "I've just been reading your very remarkable statement. . . . Do you mind if I ask you a few more questions about it?"

"Go ahead," I said.

He started in and asked me a lot of questions, going right back to my first visit to Embery Staithe. They were mostly to do with minor points that he wanted cleared up, but it took him quite a while.

Finally, he gave a satisfied nod.

"Well," he said, "you and your wife seem to have been conducting yourselves in a highly unorthodox manner—but it seems that between you you've pulled off something quite extraordinary."

At that, I relaxed. For the first time, they were unmistakably on my side.

"I've some news for you," he said. "This morning, in view of what Inspector Burns told us on the phone, we decided to search William Ellis's house. . . . You weren't mistaken about him. We found conclusive proof that he's been a prosperous professional blackmailer for many years."

I thought of Carol. How right she'd been in almost every detail!

"He kept his stuff in a wall safe on the top floor," Dobson went on. "The contents included a variety of documents and letters relating to forty-three different victims—some of them quite well-known people! We also found nearly twenty thousand pounds in cash."

I gave a low whistle.

"Yes—he was in business in a *really* big way—and of course that explains why he resorted to murder. It wasn't just a few years' freedom that he stood to lose

when his hold on Ramsden went—it was his whole liveli-
hood, everything he'd built up. He killed to keep what
he had—which was plenty! ''

I nodded. One more gap in the puzzle had been filled
—the real strength of the motive.

'' What about Ramsden? '' I asked. '' Was there
anything about him in the safe? ''

'' Yes—there was a letter. I thought you'd probably
like to see it, so I brought a photostat copy along.''
Dobson extracted the facsimile from his brief-case and
passed it across to me. The letter had been written on
the notepaper of a hotel in the Scilly Isles, and was
dated 12th April, 1946. I ran my eye quickly down it.
It said:

'' If, as you told me on the telephone last night, you
were watching from another part of the cliff and saw
what happened, you must know that there is nothing
I can say in mitigation. But since you ask me for my
version before you decide whether to speak or not, here
it is. We were fooling on the cliff top, not thinking of
danger—and suddenly my wife lost her balance and
went sprawling backwards over the edge into the sea.
I looked down and saw her in the water—she was
trying to swim but she was being swept backwards and
forwards in a narrow inlet. I managed to find a way
down the rocks to the beach. I could see her a few
yards out—she was still struggling in the foam, but
only feebly. There was swirling water everywhere and
an awful noise—it was a hellish place. I have always
been afraid of the sea. I stood there, as you saw—
completely paralysed with fear. I *wanted* to go in and
help her, but I simply couldn't force myself to move—not

at first. And then, of course, it was too late—she'd
disappeared. . . . I think I could have saved her, even
though I can't swim. The water looked deep, but
I found out later that it wasn't, it was just rough. I am
almost out of my mind with grief and shame and I
hardly care what happens to me now. The memory
of it will be with me for ever—a lifelong punishment.
I deserve every moment of it. But if you decide that
you must tell what you saw, others will suffer too—
especially my father. It was as much for his sake as
for mine that I pretended I'd done all I could to save
her, when they asked me about it. So if you can
possibly bring yourself to keep silent, I implore you
to do so. Arthur Ramsden."

So there it was—Arthur's secret, the last link in the
chain. An act of almost unbelievable cowardice. To let
your young wife drown before your eyes without lifting
a finger to help her. . . . Without even *trying* . . . ! It
was hard to imagine anything more contemptible—or
more dreadful to look back on. . . .
For a while, I sat without speaking. The truth had
never for an instant crossed my mind—yet now that I
knew it, it explained the pattern of Arthur's life as nothing
else could have done. It was easy now to understand his
moodiness, his appearance of misanthropy in those early
years, his withdrawn but furiously active existence. A
man of sensitivity and conscience, he must have lived
through a private hell, loathing and reviling himself for
the moment of cowardice that could never be undone.
For that, I felt sure, was all it had been—a moment of
panic seizure, of moral cramp. Most of his life he'd been
anything but a coward. He could so easily have sunk into

futile remorse—but he hadn't. Instead, he'd set to
work to try and rehabilitate himself in his own eyes. He'd
thrown himself into the battle with his Dartmoor farm—
and won it. He'd faced up to his diabetes with courage,
and virtually mastered that. He'd done everything he
could to prove himself. At Embery Staithe he'd even
forced himself to sail, to go bathing, to take to the water
which he hated and feared. There'd been no lack of fibre
there. By the time he'd met Fay, his self-reinstatement
must have been far advanced—and her love and admiration could have completed it. Then, out of the blue, the
fifteen-year-old incident had been flung at him again.
Ellis would have threatened to tell Fay about it. No
wonder Arthur had been so preoccupied, so fitfully
gloomy, so difficult, when we'd been there! No wonder
he'd looked at Fay so wistfully, so hungrily. . . .

Of course, I thought, he could have escaped from Ellis
simply by telling her the truth himself. It would have
been a hard confession—but if she'd been as fond of him
as she'd appeared to be, he could surely have counted on
her pity and her help. His moment of panic would have
been easily understood—and forgiven—by a woman who
loved him. . . . But pity, no doubt, would have been the
last thing he'd have wanted from Fay—pity for his weakness. He'd have wanted her respect, like any other whole
man. The respect that he needed more than anything
else in the world, the respect he'd worked for and gained.
It had been the loss of that, presumably, that he hadn't
been able to contemplate. I could understand it, up to
a point. But only up to a point. . . .

In silence, I handed the photostat back.

" A very unhappy business from start to finish," Dobson
said.

I nodded.

" I suppose," he went on, " we'll never know exactly what happened in the Scilly Isles—though it's possible to make a rough guess. Ellis would have been quite a young man at the time, so I should think this might well have been his first venture into blackmail. As I see it, he'd have witnessed the fall from the cliff and Ramsden's failure to go to his wife's help quite by chance. With his type of mind, he'd have seen the possibilities in it, especially after Ramsden had publicly committed himself to a lie about what had happened. He'd have read in the newspapers that Ramsden had a well-to-do father, and that would have encouraged him. He'd have telephoned and asked for Ramsden's comments, to get some evidence in writing—which Ramsden, too distraught to think of the dangers, supplied. He'd have appointed a place where the letter was to be delivered. You'll have noticed that it wasn't addressed to anyone by name—Ramsden obviously didn't know his identity. . . . After that there'd have been a telephoned request for a sum of money, which Ramsden in desperation would have paid or promised. Poor devil!—it isn't hard to imagine the state he'd have been in. . . ."

" And then Ellis would have faded out? " I said.

" He'd have had to, wouldn't he? Once he'd failed to come forward with his evidence at the inquest, he could hardly have threatened to produce it later—not to the authorities, anyway. I suppose he might have made another demand or two before Ramsden's father died— but after that he wouldn't have had a sufficient lever. My guess is that he didn't—that he filed the letter away and started to cultivate other victims who had more at stake. He'd have got a taste for blackmail by then—

decided it was easy and profitable. It wouldn't have been till Arthur Ramsden's second marriage that *he'd* have come back into the picture again. . . ."

" How would Ellis have known about that? "

" Well, if Fay Ramsden was on the stage the marriage must have got a bit of publicity in the newspapers. Ellis would have read about it—blackmailers of his type always watch the papers. He'd have remembered Ramsden, dug out the old letter, realised the fresh financial possibilities if Ramsden had kept the secret from his new wife, and—perhaps after waiting a while for the marriage to settle down—come up here to investigate. A telephone call to Ramsden would have been enough to establish that the secret *had* been kept and that, in the new set-up, Ramsden was prepared to start paying again rather than have it made known. Then all the rest would have followed. . . ."

I nodded slowly, and fell silent again. Perhaps we were as near the whole truth now as we were ever likely to get—yet I wasn't entirely satisfied.

" You know," I said, after a moment, " I can understand how Arthur came to pay blackmail money in the first place—he was young, naïve, scared—what with the loss of his wife and his sense of guilt he must have been in a frightful state. . . . But he got over that. He took himself in hand. He started to show character and guts. He knew he'd been weak and he was determined not to be again. I remember him saying to me once, ' Life's a struggle, isn't it?—if you give in, you've had it.' It wasn't exactly an original remark, but he said it with such feeling—it was like a summing up of his experience, a truth that he'd built into his life. . . . I find it hard to understand how a man who'd learned that lesson could have cracked so completely when Ellis showed up the second time."

"Once weak, always weak, I suppose," Dobson said. "If he thought his happiness was at stake . . ."

"What happiness could he have expected while he was in the toils of a blackmailer? He'd never have known a minute's peace again. And those night walks were already affecting his marriage. . . . It just doesn't make sense."

Dobson shrugged. "Well, it happened . . . I suppose anything seemed better than his wife knowing. He just couldn't face the humiliation."

"He'd naturally have gone to great lengths to keep the truth from her if he could," I said, "but I wouldn't have expected him to knuckle under to Ellis as easily as he did. . . . It still seems to me to be out of character."

"What else could he have done—without risking his secret?"

"He could have put up some sort of fight, I'd have thought. . . . After all, Ellis couldn't have known the strength of his new hold—not till he'd tested it. He couldn't have been sure Arthur would pay rather than have his wife told. He'd have had to feel his way. And if he'd met resistance, he wouldn't have been in a very strong position himself. Suppose Arthur had tried to bargain with him—suppose he'd said something like, ' If you'll drop this I won't do anything about you, but otherwise I'll denounce you as a blackmailer whatever the consequences'? Would Ellis have dared to take the risk?"

"Ramsden couldn't have denounced him," Dobson said, "because he didn't know who he was."

Momentarily, I'd lost sight of that. "Even so," I said,

" Arthur needn't have thrown in his hand straight away.
. . . He could have played for time, and tried to find out
who Ellis was."

" How? "

" Well, he could have stayed around at the place where
he was supposed to put the money, the way Fay did later,
until the blackmailer came to collect it—and then had
a showdown."

" He could if he'd had that sort of courage."

" He'd been trying to prove to himself for fifteen years
that he had courage. This would have been his chance
to clinch it."

Dobson grunted. " It wouldn't have been very practical, would it? For all he knew, he'd have had to wait
all night before his man showed up—perhaps all the next
night, too. I know Mrs. Ramsden didn't have to wait
very long, as it happened, but Ramsden couldn't have
been sure. And with his wife in the house, he couldn't
possibly have stayed out indefinitely without giving any
explanation."

It came to me then, in a flash. " But Arthur tried his
best to get Fay *away* from the house," I said. " I remember now. He tried to persuade her to come and spend
some time with us in London. She refused at first, but
she would have come later. . . . His reasons were very
vague, too—he just said it would be good for them. . . .
Superintendent, perhaps Arthur *was* working for a showdown. He could have made up his mind when Ellis
rang up. He could have said he'd pay, just to keep him
quiet in the meantime. He could have paid once or twice,
and stayed around in the sandhills as long as he dared,
hoping the blackmailer would turn up. Then, when Fay
started to follow him, queering his pitch, and things

began to get difficult at home, he'd have decided the only way to make sure of a meeting was to send Fay off. The first time it didn't work—but he'd have tried again, and in the end it would have worked. That way, he might have hoped to clear the whole thing up without telling his secret and without being always at the mercy of a blackmailer."

Dobson pondered. " Well—it's possible. . . ."

" I think it's more than possible," I said. " I believe it's true."

He nodded slowly. " At least no one can ever prove you wrong," he said.

We left it at that.

One thing I knew—whether I was right or wrong, I hadn't the least desire to sit in judgment on Arthur. I would remember him with affection for his considerateness and gentleness, for his kindness to me, for his long, brave struggle against daunting odds. At the worst, he'd been the victim of a single, fatal moment, and of his own nature. At the best, he'd been well on the road to redeeming himself by his own efforts. It wasn't his fault that all had ended in tragedy—and that Fay had finally shared in the tragedy too. . . . Poor Fay!

Dobson was beginning to pack up his brief-case. " Well, Mr. Renison, that seems to be about all for the moment. . . . I'm afraid some pretty bad mistakes have been made in this case, but on the information available at the time they could hardly have been avoided. . . ."

" No," I said. " For that matter, I've made a few myself! "

" At least you can count on us to give all the co-operation we can in seeing that things are put right now. . . ."

" Thank you."

" It'll take a little time, I expect—but we'll be keeping in touch with you. . . . Now you'd probably like to get away—I expect you'll be wanting to see your wife and discuss it all with her."

" I would if I knew where she was," I said.

Dobson gave me a wry look. " Oh, I can tell you that. She's probably still at Gerald Road Police Station."

I stared at him. " What's she doing there? "

" She's under arrest—or was earlier to-day, at any rate."

" For what, in heaven's name? "

" For trying to break into the basement of William Ellis's house in the early hours of this morning," Dobson said. " A neighbour gave the alarm and a patrol car picked her up. . . ." He smiled. " However, in view of what's happened since, I don't imagine we shall press the charge. She'll be home when you get there, Mr. Renison. She'll know everything by then—and she'll be expecting you. Good-bye—and good luck! "

CHAPTER XXXII

ALL THE way back, I wondered what I would say to her, and what she would say to me. She'd come out of it all so much better than I had. I felt humbled by her faith and loyalty and indomitable spirit. I wasn't at all sure that my final desperate action on the Far Sands would redeem me in her eyes or make up for the doubt and distrust I'd shown. Could our relationship ever be repaired? We certainly knew each other now—we'd something substantial to build on, if only we could start afresh. . . . But had I hurt her too much? When, three hours later, I put my key in the latch, I could scarcely control the wild hammering of my heart.

I needn't have worried. She was in the hall before I had the door open. She looked just like the Carol I'd married. The curtain of reserve had gone, and all the coldness. Tears glistened in her eyes. She said, " Darling —oh, *darling*, are you all right . . . ? "

I took her in my arms.